Not only was he a competent, attractive man who looked good in his buttoned-up clothes, but Wyatt Dawson seemed inherently decent.

He hadn't once condescended to her or made her feel like a nuisance. Quite the opposite. He was warm, easygoing and seemingly determined to put her mind at ease.

Fixing her most serene smile in place, she rose and offered him her hand to shake. "Thank you...Wyatt. I appreciate both your diligence and your kind words."

He bobbed his head, then backed away. "I'll get out of your hair. If I hear anything, I'll call." He stepped into the hall but made no move toward the building's entrance.

"Is there something else?" she asked.

He didn't bother to hide his sheepish smile. "I guess I don't need to remind you to lock up."

"No, but you can stand there and listen as I do." She flashed a quick, shaky smile. "Good night, Special Agent Dawson."

He inclined his head and mimicked touching the brim of a hat. "Good night, Ms. Beckett."

SHADOWING
HER STALKER

MAGGIE WELLS

INTRIGUE

To my adopted home state and all the Arkansans who have made me one of their own—even if I still sound like I'm "not from around here." Thank you for sharing the beauty of the Natural State with me.

Harlequin® INTRIGUE™

Recycling programs for this product may not exist in your area.

ISBN-13: 978-1-335-45718-9

Shadowing Her Stalker

Harlequin Enterprises ULC
22 Adelaide St. West, 41st Floor
Toronto, Ontario M5H 4E3, Canada
www.Harlequin.com

Printed in Lithuania

MIX
Paper | Supporting responsible forestry
FSC® C021394

By day, **Maggie Wells** is buried in spreadsheets. At night, she pens tales of intrigue and people tangling up the sheets. She has a weakness for hot heroes and happy endings. She is the product of a charming rogue and a shameless flirt, and you only have to scratch the surface of this mild-mannered married lady to find a naughty streak a mile wide.

Books by Maggie Wells

Harlequin Intrigue

Arkansas Special Agents: Cyber Crime Division

Shadowing Her Stalker

Arkansas Special Agents

Ozarks Missing Person
Ozarks Double Homicide
Ozarks Witness Protection

A Raising the Bar Brief

An Absence of Motive
For the Defense
Trial in the Backwoods

Foothills Field Search

Visit the Author Profile page at Harlequin.com.

CAST OF CHARACTERS

Cara Beckett—Millionaire lifestyle guru. Face, voice and cofounder of the LYYF app, a tech company poised to go public. She has recently been doxed, and the harassment she's faced as a woman in tech has morphed into real-life threats and attempts to harm her.

Wyatt Dawson—Special agent with the Arkansas State Police Cyber Crime Division. Wyatt is tasked with protecting Cara and tracking down whoever is terrorizing her while she takes refuge in her home state.

Elizabeth (Betsy) and James Beckett—Cara's parents. Owners of a successful family cattle farm in the foothills of the Ozark Mountains.

Chris Sharpe and Tom Wasinski—Cara's partners and the tech geniuses behind the LYYF app. When the stock goes public, all three partners stand to make a fortune beyond their wildest dreams.

Zarah Parvich—Cara's virtual assistant. Based in California, Zarah is a key resource for both Cara and Wyatt, since she has access to almost every facet of Cara's personal and professional life.

Chapter One

Most of her life Cara Beckett dreamed of being one of those actors who had to wear a disguise to get through an airport undetected. Yet, here she was—rich, famous in a way she never imagined and completely incognito as she walked through Little Rock's Bill and Hillary Clinton National Airport dressed in soft, faded jeans and a flowing white tunic.

When she booked her flight, it hadn't even registered she'd be traveling on October 31. She'd been too wrapped up in thoughts of getting out of California to notice anything different at LAX. Then, when she changed planes in Dallas, a woman who was either dressed as a witch or channeling her inner sorceress sat down across the aisle from her in the first-class cabin. As the other passengers boarded, she noted at least three men dressed as a high-profile European soccer coach, a couple teenagers in full pop star mode and multiple women wearing sweaters or appliquéd sweatshirts with pumpkin or fall motifs. She'd forgotten all about Halloween.

For the first time in a week, she breathed easy. She was definitely not in LA anymore.

The young woman working the rental counter was wearing a wedding dress with strategically placed rips and tears and a smattering of bright red paint Cara supposed was meant to be blood. Her heart lodged in her throat as she inched closer to the counter. She was glad the girl didn't know actual blood was darker. Thicker. And definitely didn't smell like craft paint.

One week ago, Cara found out her personal information—full name, address and mobile phone number—had been posted on a forum favored by self-proclaimed tech wizards. Not being a techie herself, she'd never heard of the message board, nor had she thought the breach of privacy would turn out to be a real threat. She'd thought the doxing was puzzling. At first, she was annoyed. She couldn't figure out why anyone would care who she was or where she lived. She wasn't truly a big shot in the tech sector.

But her lack of industry credibility was exactly what angered the people coming after her. And in the last week they'd gone beyond angry to terrifying.

Someone attacked her neighbor Nancy as she walked her dog two nights ago. Nancy had paused to let her Pomeranian, Buster, use the tiny patch of meticulously maintained lawn in front of Cara's Los Feliz property as his toilet, though Cara had expressly asked her not to. Cara found Nancy sprawled on the grass bleeding from stab wounds to her abdomen and side with her ever-faithful Buster barking his head off.

Nancy would recover, thank goodness, but the incident had left Cara shaken. She didn't become truly terrified until detectives looking into the stabbing showed up at Cara's door the night before asking if she had reason to believe someone would wish to harm her. They believed she had been the intended target. According to Nancy's statements to the police, her assailant had called the name "Cara" when he jumped from the passenger seat of a nondescript gray sedan. He'd also repeatedly said, "Breathe in life," while stabbing poor Nancy.

"Now, go out there and breathe in LYYF," was the tagline

Cara said at the end of each lesson or meditation offered by the app she'd helped create.

To some in the tech world, she was an actress who lucked into doing free voice-over work. They believed Chris Sharpe and Tom Wasinski were the geniuses behind LYYF, the life-style and social application downloaded on over seven hundred million mobile devices each year. She was simply the face. And the voice. Few would call her the key to the app's success, though the truth was, the business hadn't been going anywhere until she'd stepped in.

At times she wished she never had.

Curling her lips in, she bit down, breathing deep and evenly through her nose. She needed to keep her anxiety at bay for now. In ninety minutes, give or take, she'd be safe at home with her parents. All she had to do was get in a car and drive. Soon she'd be about as far from Los Angeles as a person could be—mentally, if not geographically. Far from a world where people measured every success against their own failures. In a place where internet and cellular service were both still spotty and the residents had more important things to worry about than whether they had Wi-Fi available 24-7.

Ahead of her, a man argued with the rental agent. Apparently the largest vehicle available was a midsize sedan and they'd reserved an SUV. She glanced over and saw a harried woman trying to keep track of three kids under the age of ten. Cara smiled sympathetically. It was clear both mother and father were fighting a losing battle.

When he finally stepped aside, resigned to shoehorning his family into the available Hyundai, she took her place at the counter with a wan smile. Holding up her phone so the agent could scan her reservation, she said, "I'll take whatever you have."

The young woman pulled up the reservation, asked Cara to answer the rental agreement questions on the tablet mounted to the counter and, with a relieved smile, offered her a map of the area.

Cara waved it away. "No, thank you. I know where I'm headed."

"You can choose whichever car you like from section 104," the agent said as she slipped a printed ticket into a sleeve and wrote "104" across the front in black marker. "Thank you and Happy Halloween."

Cara took the paperwork from her. "Thanks," she replied tiredly.

Making sure her massive leather tote was still riding securely atop her roller bag, she wheeled out of the line. The man behind her stepped up, peering closely at his phone, thumb scrolling frantically. "Hang on," she heard him say to the clerk. "I can't find my reservation email."

Should have used the app, Cara thought as she strode toward the exit.

She spotted a ladies' room and decided to stop. She had a long drive ahead and too much coffee in her system. After washing her hands, she flicked a few drops of cold water at her face in hopes of freshening up. By the time she exited, she saw a brown-haired man dressed in the Midwestern male uniform of khaki pants and a polo shirt making a beeline for section 104. There were only two cars parked there—identical silver subcompacts.

She smiled as he slowed to a halt behind her. "Should we flip a coin?" she asked.

He shook his head, but barely glanced in her direction as he held out a hand. "Ladies first."

"Thanks."

Too worn out to do anything but keep moving, Cara approached the vehicle on the left. Not bothering with the trunk, she stowed her roller bag in the back seat, then tossed her tote into the wheel well on the passenger side. The fob for the ignition was in the cup holder. She put her foot on the brake and pressed the button and the engine purred to life.

She saw the man move to the driver's side of the rental beside hers as she pulled her door shut. Mentally mapping her route out of Little Rock, she was fastening her seat belt when the passenger door opened and the khaki-clad man dropped into the seat beside her.

"Don't scream, no one's around anyhow," he said in a gruff whisper.

Wide-eyed, she stared at the gleaming weapon pointed at her. *Gunmetal gray*, her brain supplied unhelpfully. She looked up to find her new passenger had pulled a safety-orange balaclava down over his head and topped it with a leaf-and-twig-printed cap.

A flash of a long-forgotten trip to the feed store with her father came to mind. Home from California for Thanksgiving, she'd been about the only person in town not dressed in forest browns and bright orange. Her father had cracked himself up musing about how camouflage was never more effective than in the fall in Arkansas.

It was true. Too true.

"What do you want?" She pointed a trembling finger at the tote half-crushed under his feet. "There's cash in my wallet. Take it. Take what you need."

The man gave a derisive snort. "I am taking what I need. Now drive, or I'll shoot you right here."

In the moment, the notion of being left for dead in a sub-compact rental parked in section 104 of a nearly deserted parking deck sounded like the worst possible fate. So she shifted into gear, and pulled out of the space.

"Where do you want me to go?"

"Get us out of here," he ordered.

She chanced a glance at her passenger as she pointed the car toward the exit. No, she hadn't imagined the gun. Or the khakis. Or the polo shirt. But even if she could describe them down to the weave of the cotton of his shirt, the police would still be looking for a needle in a haystack.

There was absolutely nothing notable about the man beside her.

Cara eased out of the parking deck and into the lane leading to the airport exit. There'd be a gate to clear. Someone would see them. She'd be able to get help.

Consoling herself with the knowledge they were in a well-populated area, she headed for the parking attendant. But as they rolled to a stop behind another car, she saw none of the white booths with their sliding glass windows were manned.

To her horror, she saw the velvet-cloaked arm of the wizard family patriarch wave his rental agreement at a scanner attached to the side of the booth. The electronic gate lifted, and the overstuffed sedan rolled away.

When Cara pulled up to the booth, she gazed up into its emptiness in bewilderment. The man beside her bumped her elbow. She jumped and looked down. Had he nudged her with the gun? No. His hand. He shoved the rental envelope she'd tucked into her tote at her.

"Stop messing around," he growled.

She blinked back a hot rush of frustrated tears as she took the sleeve bearing the printed barcode and held it up to the scanner.

The barrier lifted, but she couldn't seem to take her foot off the brake.

"Drive," her abductor ordered.

"Drive where?"

He turned in his seat to square up with her, the gun clutched in his right hand. "Go. Now."

He uttered the commands through clenched teeth, and Cara's brain engaged. She hit the gas and the small car lurched forward, engine revving. The road leading away from the single-terminal airport was nearly deserted. As she approached the entrance to the major arteries surrounding the capital city, she instinctively lifted her foot from the gas.

"Take the ramp," he ordered.

She put on her signal, but took the right turn at a high rate of speed. Cara chanced a glance at her passenger. He gripped the console between the seats to keep his equilibrium, but kept his weapon pointed in her direction.

The bypass ended a few miles from the airport, one lane leading to downtown Little Rock and Interstate 40. She gravitated toward it, intent on following the route to her parents' ranch in a snug valley of the Ozark Mountains, but the man beside her had a different plan.

"Stay in the middle lane," he instructed.

"But—" she began to protest.

"Middle lane," he repeated, cutting her off as an eighteen-wheeler forced its way out of the merge lane, neatly boxing her in.

She followed the flow of traffic onto Interstate 30 South. The other lane circled the south side of the city on its way to Texas. Cara's mind raced across the miles ahead. She wasn't overly familiar with the southwest corner of the state. She'd never been to Texarkana or any of the other towns between Little Rock and Dallas. And the only times she'd been to Dallas, she'd flown.

"Where are we going?" she asked, speaking only to fill the silence. Perhaps, if she got him talking—

"We're going to drive until I tell you to stop."

She gripped the steering wheel tighter, her knuckles glowing white against her skin. "You can take the car. I don't care," she offered. "Take it."

"I am," he said, a note of smug amusement in his tone. "And I'm taking you with it."

His insouciance annoyed her, but she kept her eyes glued to the traffic ahead of her. The last thing she needed was to tick off the man with the gun. Traffic was light as they raced past the small bedroom communities flanking the highway on the other side of the county line.

They flew past strip malls and chain restaurants, budget hotels and car dealerships. Logic told her the thriving commercial areas denoted miles of civilization beyond. They were driving through what passed for urban sprawl in a sparsely populated state. But it wouldn't last long. Soon, there wouldn't be anything but large tracts of forest dotted with tiny towns. Sleepy, slightly run-down communities with a post office, possibly a diner or barbecue joint and, if they were lucky, a gas station.

Sure enough, shopping centers gave way to a few edge-of-town motels. A billboard advertised a travel plaza at the next exit. Green highway signs listed the mileage to Hot Springs, Arkadelphia and Texarkana.

As the highway narrowed to two lanes in each direction, Cara forced herself to take three deep, deliberate breaths, counting in her head as she cycled through each one.

"There you go, breathe in life," the man beside her said, his voice faintly mocking.

Cara's blood ran ice-cold.

Breathe in life. Breathe in LYYF. She'd ended every recording she'd ever done for the LYYF app with those soothing words.

Now they terrified her.

The guy who'd pointed a gun at her in an airport parking deck had twisted them. Taunted her with words meant to reassure. He knew who she was. This wasn't some random carjacking. Had he been waiting for her. Why? This could not be happening.

Clutching the steering wheel, she turned to look at him, wide-eyed. "What did you say?"

"You heard me," he answered, waving her disbelief away.

"You know who I am?"

She cringed as the words came out of her mouth, but her brain was blown and she wasn't feeling up to playing cat and mouse. What was the use when the cat was holding her at gunpoint.

"Do you buy into all the woo-woo meditation stuff, or do you do it because they pay you to say it?"

He sat there pointing a gun at her and he expected her to answer questions about her job?

She clenched her jaw as one of the three semis boxing her in decided he wanted to work his way into the right lane. She slowed to avoid being clipped as the big rig edged over. A sign advertising a gas station with a fast-food franchise flashed past her window. The truck ahead of her slowed. Cara looked to her right and spotted the brightly lit station.

The driver ahead of her sped up as they approached the ramp. Cara accelerated too, but when she checked her mirror, she saw the semi on her rear bumper was signaling his intent to exit.

They were almost past the ramp when Cara jerked the wheel hard to the right, throwing her passenger against the door.

The tires kicked up loose gravel from the shoulder.

The man beside her cursed a blue streak.

The driver behind them indicated his displeasure by blowing his horn at her.

A trailer hauling wood chips sat stationary at the bottom of the ramp, right turn signal flashing. Cross traffic on the county road at the bottom of the ramp did not let up.

"What do you think you're doing?" the man holding the gun yelled, reaching across to grab the steering wheel.

Cara jammed on the brakes, her arms locked against the steering wheel to counteract the laws of physics. Her passenger boomeranged into the dash. Behind them, brakes screamed in protest and the driver laid on his horn.

The moment they jerked to a halt, she thrust the gearshift into Park, popped the latch on her seat belt and rolled out the driver's door onto the gritty berm.

The man shouted, but she didn't look back.

She ran.

Cara ran flat out, streaking down along the side of the trailer filled with fragrant wood shavings. Oblivious to the drama playing out behind him, the driver let off his brakes enough to make the hydraulics sigh with anticipation. Cara skidded into the ditch running alongside the ramp, thanking the stars above she'd had sense enough to wear sneakers for the plane ride.

She watched as the truck crept forward a few feet, then jerked to a stop again. Glancing behind her, she saw a battered pickup hurtling down the county road. She heard another shout, followed by a terrifying pop.

Cara didn't wait for the man to get a second round off. Using the pickup as cover, she darted across the ramp in front of the semi, praying the driver wasn't tempted to inch any farther into the intersection.

Breathless, she slid down the slope on the other side of the ramp. Peeking over tall grass, she saw her passenger sliding behind the wheel.

Flattening herself in the damp grass, she held her breath as she heard the rev of engines. Another blast of impatient honking told her the driver stuck behind her abandoned rental had had enough shenanigans for one day. Seconds later, she heard the rumble and sigh of air brakes again.

Cara raised her head enough to peer over the edge of the culvert. Beyond the beams of a tractor hauling a flatbed filled with spooled steel, she saw the taillights of a silver subcompact flash as it sped up the entrance ramp on the opposite side of the country road.

He was taking off without her.

Relief pulsed through her veins.

He was gone.

Panting, Cara lowered her head to rest on the backs of her trembling hands. Cold dampness seeped into the knees of her jeans. Her palms throbbed. She had no doubt she'd find them speckled with glass and gravel from her dive for safety, but she didn't care.

He was gone.

She was alive.

She was safe.

"Breathe in life," she murmured. And she did. She drank in the cool, damp air until her lungs were full to bursting, and held it there.

Then, a pair of battered boots tramped down the grass right in front of her. Every oxygen molecule she'd ingested exploded out of her when a man spoke.

"Do you have some kind of death wish or something, lady?"

Chapter Two

Wyatt Dawson didn't mind working late. Truthfully, he preferred the office after hours. Because they were a small team, most of the members of the cybercrime division took work home with them, but he liked the time in the office alone. He wasn't antisocial, though some would say he was; it was more that he liked the idea of keeping his work at work.

And he was so close to zeroing in on a solid lead.

Sitting at his desk with his feet up, he was scanning lines of data, looking for the IP address needed to confirm his suspicions. If he could connect the dots, all the extra hours would pay off. The spot on the multiagency task force investigating the sale and movement of illegally produced distilled spirits through northwest Arkansas would be his. He was close. He could taste it. So close he was tempted to ignore the ringing desk phone.

But he couldn't. The cybercrime division was still in its infancy. He and his tiny group of talented colleagues were on a mission to prove their worth to the Department of Public Safety. And because they were worthy, he would take the call. Even though it was after hours.

Even though it meant shifting mental gears at the precise moment he needed them locked on target.

He frowned as the desk phone continued to pester him.

The short two-tone ring indicated an intraoffice phone call. The last thing he needed was for someone on the inside to insinuate they weren't pulling their weight. Dropping his feet to the floor, he reached for the receiver of the desk phone and wedged it between his ear and shoulder.

"CCD, Dawson here," he said as he typed a note into his spreadsheet to mark where he'd left off.

"Agent Dawson? This is Trooper Chad Masterson," the caller said with brisk efficiency. "I have a sort of unusual circumstance unfolding here, and I'm wondering if you might be able to help me."

Wyatt shook his mouse to keep the computer from transitioning into sleep mode then sat up straighter in his chair and took hold of the receiver. "Happy to. How can I help?"

"Have you ever heard of a woman called Cara Beckett?" the trooper asked.

Scowling, Wyatt picked up a pen and jotted the name on a pad of sticky notes he kept beside the phone. The name did ring a bell, but he found the man's coy approach annoying. He wasn't a big fan of fishing expeditions whether they employed a line and hook, or clumsily delivered yes or no questions.

"I'm gonna need a little more than a name," he informed his colleague.

"Cara Beckett," the trooper repeated. "Says she works for a company called LYYF. Spelled with two *Y*'s. *L-Y-Y-F*." Masterson was unable to mask the disdain in his voice as he spelled out the company name. "I believe it's some kind of phone application."

Wyatt sighed. The number of electronic troglodytes he encountered within the ranks of law enforcement never failed to amaze him. Sure, they were all for DNA matches and advanced ballistics, but tie a computer, tablet or smartphone to a crime and they bragged about how they were still using AOL as their email provider. Or pretended they hadn't heard of one of the tech world's biggest sensations.

"Yes, I'm familiar with the application," he said briskly.

Truthfully, he was more than familiar. He was a daily user. He reached for his own phone and swiped through a couple of screens, stopping when he spotted the bright orange icon with the stylized *L* at its center. The home page loaded and he stared at the photo of a woman seated in the lotus position, her eyes closed and her lips curved into a serene smile.

All the puzzle pieces fell into place.

"Cara Beckett is one of the founding partners of LYYF. It's a lifestyle and wellness application." He tapped his pen on the desk a couple of times then opened the app, anxious to put the name and face together. "You probably have it on your phone too," he informed Trooper Masterson. "Our health insurance provider gave everybody a free subscription to the service for a year as part of our benefits package a couple years ago."

"Hmm, I'm not familiar," Masterson said, unable to mask the hint of derision in his tone. "I'll have to ask my wife if she tried it. She likes all those lifestyle things." He guffawed. "I pay for the whole dang cable package, but all she ever watches is the home-makeover channel. If I come home to one more set of paint swatches I'm going to spit."

Wyatt clenched his jaw. He had to take one of the calming breaths he learned from using LYYF before posing the obvious question. "Why are you asking me about Cara Beckett?"

"From what I gather, she's some kind of celebrity."

Wyatt frowned at the descriptor. Celebrity? Maybe in some circles, but not in the way Masterson would recognize.

"Not a Hollywood celebrity, but in other circles, yeah, maybe," he conceded. "Again, why do you ask?"

"Because I got her sitting in an office down here. A trucker said she practically leaped out of a moving vehicle to get away from the guy she was ridin' with."

"Leaped out of a moving car?"

"Says she was abducted. Man with a gun jacked her rental car at the airport. The woman is pretty shaken up. No purse or phone or ID of any kind. No money. The guy who found her took her up to the truck stop and waited with her until a patrolman arrived. They brought her back here and dropped her at my desk, but I'm not quite sure what to make of her story."

"Is there a reason why you don't believe her story?" Wyatt asked.

"No particular reason," Masterson replied cautiously. "It's not something that happens around here very often."

"Oh, I'd say we see our fair share of carjackings." Wyatt himself had a friend who was lured from her car at a fast-food restaurant and left standing by as her vehicle sped away. She'd been one of the lucky ones.

"She keeps talking about somebody docking her and I'm not sure what she means." Wyatt could hear the guy scratching his head. "She seems to think there's some connection between the docking and what happened to her today. Keeps saying it can't be a coincidence."

"Docking?" Wyatt scowled as he watched the progress bar at the bottom of his screen creep toward completion. He glanced down at the name he'd scrawled on the sticky note, then zeroed in on the blinking cursor as if it might give up the answer to what was nagging him.

"What is Cara Beckett doing in Arkansas?" he whispered, talking to himself.

But Masterson answered. "Says she's from here. Folks own a place up in Searcy County. Ranchers."

"Searcy County? That's north, isn't it? They were heading south," Wyatt noted.

"I don't think this guy with the gun was hoping to meet the folks," Masterson said dryly.

Wyatt turned the information he'd been given over in his head. "Docking? I don't know what she means."

"Makes two of us. I tried to get a better answer out of her but she kept goin' on about her home address and phone number being leaked and someone called Nancy gettin' attacked outside her house. Frankly, she's a bit…overwrought," Masterson drawled.

Wyatt sat up straighter partly because he was annoyed by the trooper's supercilious attitude but mostly because he was catching on to exactly what Cara Beckett was trying to tell them.

"Do you mean doxing?" he demanded, his tone sharp.

"Excuse me?"

"Doxing." But saying the word louder didn't help it penetrate the trooper's skull. "Doxing is when somebody on the internet, usually a hacker or some kind of troll, unearths someone's personal information and publishes it for the world to see."

He paused to let the explanation sink in, but Trooper Masterson remained quiet.

"It's slang for dropping the documents on someone."

"But why? Who is she?"

"She's a partner in a tech company."

"So shouldn't she be able to stop this, uh, doxing thing?"

Wyatt rolled his eyes at the man's naivete. "Picture some internet users as a pack of rabid dogs. There are always a few who will chase after a person at the slightest provocation."

"You think this Cara Beckett person provoked this threat against her?"

"I'm not saying anything of the sort. She could simply be guilty of nothing more than breathing oxygen on a daily basis. It doesn't take much to get a few disgruntled users to go after a high profile target."

"You think her profile is high enough people would, uh, dox her? Kidnap her?" The other man sounded dubious. "I've never even heard of her."

"You follow tech trends pretty closely, Masterson?"

"I know who Jeff Bezos and Elon Musk are," he countered.

"Congratulations," Wyatt said dryly. "Listen, the lady you have sitting in an office down there might not be Bezos or Musk, but she's far wealthier than you or I can ever dream of being." He thought back to the article he'd read about the masterminds behind LYYF. "They're about to take the company public. Soon Cara Beckett's net worth will be stratospheric."

"She doesn't look like a millionaire right now," Masterson grumbled.

"Billionaire," Wyatt interjected.

"She's wearin' jeans and a plain white shirt. All muddy and stuff from rolling in the ditch. And the trucker gave her twenty dollars because she didn't have any walking-around money." Masterson added the last bit as if it was conclusive evidence against Wyatt's claims. "She's down here right now making some calls to see if she can round up a hotel or place to stay the night using a police report as ID."

Wyatt swiped at his cell until his internet browser popped up. A quick query yielded the article he had read a few days before. In it, a slim smiling young woman with chic, close-cropped blond hair and wide blue eyes beamed out at him. She stood a half step in front of the men she claimed were her two best friends from college.

There were plenty of people who thought an out-of-work actress didn't deserve the 33-percent partnership the creators of LYYF offered her in exchange for voice-over work when they were prestart-up. But they made a deal, and Cara Beckett become the voice and later, when their popular video sessions were added, the face of LYYF.

The trolls and tech bros liked to grumble about the equal partnership Chris Sharpe and Tom Wasinski had traded for her services at the beginning of their venture. But no one could deny Cara Beckett was as much a part of LYYF's success as their clever coding and attractive graphics. No amount of superior interface could have made the app a phenomenon. Her face and voice were key. As was her willingness to step out from behind the curtain and become the public spokesperson her collaborators never wanted to be.

He scrolled through the profile he'd skimmed the week before. In the article, her cofounders weren't shy about giving her the respect she deserved. Without Cara Beckett's easy, open smile and welcoming demeanor, the application wouldn't have been half the hit it was.

Glancing back at the desk phone, he noted the extension Masterson was using and rose from his chair. "Hang tight. I'll be there in a few minutes to talk to her. If even a little bit of what you say she says happened to her is true, at best we're dealing with the situation straddling multiple jurisdictions."

"And worst-case scenario?"

"The media finds out," Wyatt said grimly.

"Exactly what I'm afraid of." Masterson heaved a sigh. "Come on down. She's got nowhere else to go and no way to get there anyhow."

MASTERSON WAS EVERYTHING Wyatt expected from their conversation. Tall and not quite barrel-chested, he wore his dark hair in a high and tight buzz cut. As he drew closer and the two shook hands, Wyatt could see short strands of silver intensified the effect of the trooper's white-walled haircut. Deep creases furrowed the man's brow, and squint lines radiated from cool blue eyes. Wyatt couldn't blame the man for his natural skepticism. No doubt, the man had seen some strange things in his years of service.

Cara Beckett sat in one of the small offices on the perimeter of the bullpen. The door was closed, but the miniblinds covering the office window were drawn up. She looked different in person. It wasn't the grass-stained clothes or the smudge of mud dried on her jawline. Her hair looked softer. It was an inch or two longer than in the photos on the app, and the color was more a honey gold than beachy white-blond streaks.

She looked tired. Small. And though he knew from her yoga videos she was strong and almost rubber-band flexible, under the fluorescent lights of the Arkansas State Police Headquarters, she came across as almost unspeakably fragile.

"Have you gotten anything more from her?" Wyatt asked.

Masterson shook his head. "She just got off the phone."

Wyatt nodded, then gestured to the door. "Do you mind if I have a chat?"

Sweeping an arm toward the door, Masterson said, "Have at it. I have a call in to the rental company to try to get the information on the stolen vehicle."

With a nod, Wyatt started for the office door. He gave it a couple raps with the knuckle of his index finger, then cracked it open. Cara Beckett looked up with wide, frightened eyes.

He kept the opening to little more than a crack, but made sure to smile to show her he meant no harm. "Hello. Ms. Beckett?" She nodded, but he made no move to enter the small office. "I'm Special Agent Wyatt Dawson. I'm a member of our cybercrimes division. Trooper Masterson called me. May I speak with you for a few minutes?"

She eyed him warily. "Cybercrimes division? They have one of those here?"

He pushed the door open a few inches more, and allowed his smile to widen as well. "Anywhere the internet goes, so go the scammers."

"And the trolls," she said, bitterness edging her tone. "And the out-and-out criminals."

"May I come in?" He pointed to the chair opposite the small desk where she'd sat to use the telephone.

She inclined her head, and he caught the light bounce off the diamond studs she wore in her ears. They weren't ostentatious, but were certainly more than mere chips. As he settled in the chair he took in the gold bangles on her wrist. A delicate chain holding a pendant with a large multicolored stone encircled her throat. She wore rings on multiple fingers and one thumb, but the third finger on her left hand was bare. He filed the information away as he leaned back in the chair, assuming a pose more in line with casual conversation than interrogation.

"You don't believe the man who abducted you intended to rob you." He made it a statement, knowing it would draw more of an answer from her than a question.

She shook her head. "No. I offered him my wallet, the car, anything he wanted. He said he wanted me."

Wyatt pursed his lips, letting the words hang in the air for a minute as he formulated his next question. But before he could ask it, she shook her head.

"No, not wanted. Needed. I told him to take what he needed, and he said he was, then ordered me to drive."

Nodding, Wyatt resisted the urge to lean forward in

his chair. He didn't want to come across as aggressive. He wanted her comfortable enough to tell her story her way. To remember things as they actually happened without framing them through the lens of hindsight.

"He wasn't familiar to you at all." Again, a statement, not a question.

"It's been a long time since I've lived in Arkansas, Special Agent Daw—"

"Wyatt," he interrupted.

"Wyatt," she repeated with a nod, a small smile tugging at the corners of her mouth.

"Something funny," he asked.

"I don't run into too many Wyatts in LA."

He smirked. "Maybe not." Since she felt comfortable enough to mock him, he leaned forward, planting his elbows on his knees and clasping his hands. "May I call you Cara?"

"Yes."

"Cara, tell me about the doxing incident," he said, driving straight to his main point of interest. "Do you know what precipitated it? What fallout have you experienced? Did you feel you were in danger in California?"

She gaped at him for a moment, seemingly stunned by the abrupt shift in conversation. "I, uh, I don't know why," she managed to stammer. "I mean, there have always been, um, detractors, but no. I have no idea why someone decided to make my personal information public. And I don't know why anyone would be interested. I'm not a celebrity or anything." She opened her hands in a helpless shrug. "I'm not even an influencer."

Wyatt huffed, charmed by her naive assessment of her standing in the virtual community. "Aren't you?"

He pulled out his own phone and woke the screen. The welcome page of the LYYF app appeared, and front and center was a close-up video of Cara asking, "Are you ready to get the most from your LYYF?"

She didn't respond, but her expression hardened. "As for fallout. My address and phone were posted on a number of message boards. If you're at all familiar with the internet, you know there are some users who aren't always pleasant."

"Harassment?"

She nodded. "Mostly in-app and social media messages at first, but then they hacked my company email and things spiraled even more from there. The LAPD have been on the case. I can give you the information of the…" She paused, grimaced, then shook her head. "I had contact information in my phone, but now—"

Her phone was gone.

He watched her swallow hard and hoped she was gulping down her fear. It was hard to outrun internet harassment. Life outside of the app would be better if she gathered her resolve and found a way to stand her ground. Then again, the woman had jumped out of a car in the middle of nowhere when a man was holding a gun on her. If knowing when to bail wasn't the biggest part of taking control of one's life, he didn't know what was.

"You've never seen the man who abducted you?" he asked, shifting into lightning-round mode.

"No."

"Did he mention LYYF, or give any indication he knew who you were?"

She started to shake her head, then stopped. "Not directly. He only said the part about taking what he needed then ordered me to drive."

"But you believe the implication was you were what he was after," he concluded.

"Yes."

Wyatt nodded, then pressed on. "Did he make any sexual advances? Insinuations? Touch you in any way construed as intimate?"

"No. He didn't touch me at all." She let out a whoosh of breath. "No. Nothing, uh, sexual."

"So let's assume for now robbery and sexual assault weren't his motive." He sat up straight in the chair again, holding her gaze. "If he wasn't someone you knew or recognized, we might also shelve personal agenda."

"Personal agenda?"

"Old boyfriend, spurned lover, the guy who wanted to take you to the homecoming dance but never worked up the nerve to ask you," he said with an offhanded wave. "You tick anyone off on the plane?"

The question coaxed a short huff of a laugh out of her. "I don't think I talked to anyone."

"Hog the armrest?"

She shook her head. "Dozed most of the way here. I haven't been sleeping well."

"Who knew you were coming to Arkansas?"

She shook her head. "My assistant. I think she told my partners. The neighbor who shares my cat."

Lifting a brow, he asked, "You share a cat?"

"She's a stray. Huge commitment issues. The McNeils and I both feed her. Why settle, right?"

He gave her a wry smile. "Smart cat." Nodding to the desk phone, he asked, "Did you call your folks?"

She shook her head, but when she spoke her voice was barely more than a whisper. "No."

"No?"

She raised one shoulder in a shrug, and the ruined white shirt she wore nearly slid off her shoulder. She wore some sort of spaghetti strap tank top thing under it. Her skin was tanned to a shade lighter than a golden glow. He wondered if the color came from the sun or a booth. Or maybe she had one of those spray-on jobs done. Either way, it was definitely more California tan than the blistering burns the Arkansas sun doled out.

She tipped her chin up. "My parents didn't know I was coming. And now... I don't want my mom to worry."

Wyatt sensed there was more to the story there, but he didn't press. Shifting gears, he hooked an arm over the back of the chair. "There are some nice hotels downtown. New ones, or you could go with a classic and stay at the Capital Hotel." He bit the inside of his cheek. "Were you able to contact anyone who can help?"

She nodded. "Trooper Masterson let me call my assistant, Zarah. Thank goodness she had contact information on her website. She's having a phone delivered from the Tech-Mobile store and overnighting my passport, so I have official ID, and a credit card. I have a copy of my driver's license in cloud storage as well. I assume I can use it along with the police report, if needed." He nodded and she went on. "She also rented a condo here in town for a couple of nights. I'll get a rideshare from here once I get the phone and pick up a new rental tomorrow."

Wyatt pressed his lips together to keep from letting out a low whistle. "She sounds very efficient." It never ceased to amaze him how money could pave right over the biggest potholes in life. Still, he wasn't sure she'd thought her plan through. "Did she set the phone up from your previous account?"

Cara blinked twice. "I assume so. Why?"

He did his best to hide his grimace. With a single-word question, she'd proved the tech bros right about her lack of technological savvy. "You said you've been receiving messages from strangers either through apps or email?"

"Yes."

"Texts as well?"

"Yes."

Her eyes widened as she turned toward the window. Trooper Masterson approached the office, his expression sour as he raised his hand for them to see. A plastic bag imprinted with the TechMobile logo dangled from the tip of his index finger. The man was clearly peeved to be reduced to the role of delivery boy.

Wyatt stood and opened the door. "Thank you," he said as he relieved the older man of the parcel. "If you want to finish up with Ms. Beckett's statement, I'll get this set up for her to use."

"You don't need—" she started to say as she rose from the chair, but she stopped when Wyatt looked over to her for permission to pull the familiar box from the bag. She nodded her assent.

"I'm happy to set this up to forward any communications coming in to your number to a dummy we'll set up here. Once I'm finished, I'll talk you through how best to use it without giving too much information about your location away," he interrupted. "Then, if you'd like, I can drop you off at your rental." When she seemed taken aback by the offer, he rushed to put her at ease. "Or we can get a patrol car to take you. Rideshare apps rely on cellular signals and GPS to triangulate location. We want to avoid anyone getting a read on where you are if we can."

"You think someone will use my phone to track me?" She appeared both incredulous and horrified by the notion.

"It's the fastest way. With all the apps we rely on and

location-based services, we make it too easy," Wyatt said with a grim scowl. "But I can help you. Let me help you."

Cara Beckett scooted out from behind the desk to join Trooper Masterson in the doorway. She eyed the uniformed man for a long moment, then turned to Wyatt, taking in his flat-front khakis and checked button-down shirt.

"Thank you," she said quietly, then slipped past the trooper to head back to his desk.

Wyatt and Masterson exchanged a nod-shrug combo before the older man turned away.

The second they were gone, he unboxed the phone and powered it up. The greeting screen appeared, and a smirk twisted his lips as he zipped through the multistep setup, denying the palm-sized supercomputer access to any of Cara Beckett's information. As he continued to delete applications, deny access and ignore dire warnings, he murmured a steady stream of mumbles. "No. Nope. Bye now. Can't accept. Decline. Nope. Nuh-uh," he muttered to himself.

Once he'd pared the smartphone down to its minimal functions, he sat back, satisfied with his work. Reaching for his own phone, he dialed the number displayed in the settings. Cara's phone sprang to life. He declined the call, then saved his contact information in her empty contact list.

He'd have to go over a list of dos, don'ts, and never-evers with her. Surely she'd see the reasoning behind it all. She had to. He'd make her see. Somehow, he had to make Cara Beckett understand if she wanted to get her life back, she'd have to do so without the help of the LYYF app in the short term.

Chapter Three

Cara sat on the rock-hard sofa of the condo Zarah had secured for her and stared down at the phone Special Agent Wyatt Dawson had programmed for her. She couldn't recall the last time she'd held a device set up to have so little function in the modern world. Cara took him up on his offer to drive her to the short-term rental. She was still reeling from the events of the day and found she was more than willing to let someone else take over.

As if defying the man with the gun and taking a leap toward freedom had depleted all her decision-making capabilities.

Agent Dawson, Wyatt, had insisted on walking her to the door. He actually groaned when he spotted the bags waiting for her on the unit's welcome mat. "Who is this Zarah person?" he'd asked as he helped her carry the haul inside.

"Zarah Parvich is my assistant. Virtual assistant. She works out of her home in the San Fernando Valley."

"She's definitely on the ball."

"I'd be lost without her."

Wyatt set the bags on the condo's kitchen island, then launched into a lengthy spiel on smartphone safety. Then he proceeded to check and double-check the settings on her new device. By the time he was finished, she was looking at a phone she could only use as, well, a phone.

"I programmed my number in as well as the numbers for Masterson and the CCD extension," he said as she continued to stare at the unadorned wallpaper on the screen. "I've also set it to decline any unknown callers. I'd recommend you refrain from adding more contacts. Any call coming to this new number will go straight to voicemail."

No apps. No email. No turning the cellular signal on unless she intended to make a call, and then she was to remember to switch it off the minute she hung up. She had a new phone number, one she'd have to use to call Zarah and communicate verbally if she was getting the gist of Agent Dawson's instructions.

"Assume everything is compromised," he told her. "For the time being, write things down."

He gestured to the spiral-bound notebook Zarah had shipped with the bags of food, toiletries and a wardrobe of leggings, T-shirts and zippered hoodies. Zarah knew Cara well enough to include a journal. Cara was a big fan of journaling and often encouraged others to dump their concerns onto the page.

She tried not to think about the notebook tucked into her carry-on bag. All her innermost thoughts and worries were riding around with a kidnapper. Possibly fodder for ongoing stalking.

"Do you think it would be okay to connect to the Wi-Fi here?" Wyatt nodded slowly, and Cara could practically feel the tug of his reluctance. "What?"

"I downloaded a more secure browser. It's the one with the fireball icon. Use it instead of the default." He went on, rambling about how Wi-Fi connections in public spaces where log-in was not required would be best from a security standpoint. He mentioned fast-food restaurants, coffee shops or stores, but cautioned her against attempting to log into any of her social media accounts. "Oh, and be sure to clear your cache when you're done."

She nodded. "Thank you. I will."

Wyatt clapped his hands together, then rubbed his palms. "Okay, then. You'll be all right here?"

His obvious reluctance to leave her alone in this strange place touched her. "I will be."

He walked to the window and peered down into the complex's parking area. "It's a weeknight, so there shouldn't be much trouble."

"I'll call if there are any issues." Wyatt scraped his palms down his pants as he turned back. He looked…nervous. "Is there something you're not telling me?"

"Nothing. Uh—" he flashed a weak smile "—I, um, I wanted to say… You should know…"

When he petered out without actually saying a damn thing, she set the stripped-down phone aside and rose to her feet. "I should know what?"

He shook his head, holding up his hands in futile surrender. "Nothing bad. I was only… I use your app."

The words came out in such a rush it took Cara a moment to process them. "Wha— Oh. Oh… You do?"

"Yes." He wet his lips, then gave a vigorous nod. "Actually, I know a few people who do. They made a free trial part of our healthcare package a couple years ago, and well, I'm a fan." He tossed the last off with a dismissive little laugh. "Ponied up for my own subscription."

But Cara wasn't inclined to dismiss anyone who appreciated her work. "Wow. I'm flattered. And so gratified you find it helpful."

"Very helpful."

She wanted to ask what he liked best. Wanted to know if he was in it for the finance or life coaching, like most men claimed, or if he stuck around because he found some benefit in the wellness practices. Or had he—as the fouler emails and messages she'd received implied—found a more prurient solace while watching her videos or listening to her voice?

She didn't want to know.

Not only was he a competent, attractive man who looked good in his buttoned-up clothes, but also because, like the truck driver who'd coaxed her out of the ditch and made sure she was delivered into safe hands, Wyatt Dawson seemed inherently decent. He didn't seem to be infected with the sort of Southern-fried misogyny Trooper Masterson and so many of the young men she'd known growing up were steeped in. He hadn't once condescended to her, or made her feel like a nuisance. Quite the opposite. He was warm, easygoing and seemingly determined to put her mind at ease.

Fixing her most serene smile in place, she rose and offered him her hand to shake. "Thank you… Wyatt. I appreciate both your diligence and your kind words."

He bobbed his head, then backed away. "I'll get out of your hair. If I hear anything, I'll call."

"Thank you again," she said.

He stepped into the hall, but made no move toward the building's entrance.

"Is there something else?" she asked.

He didn't bother to hide his sheepish smile. "I guess I don't need to remind you to lock up."

"No, but you can stand there and listen as I do." She flashed a quick, shaky smile. "Good night, Special Agent Dawson."

He inclined his head and mimicked touching the brim of a hat. "Good night, Ms. Beckett."

She closed the heavy door between them, then made a racket of engaging the locks before moving to the electronic alarm panel. It was set up differently from the one at her home, so she took a moment to scan the printed instructions the unit's owner had framed beside it.

"Don't forget there's an alarm," he called from the other side of the door.

"I'm doing it now," she called back. "Jeez. Give a person a minute."

"Sorry."

The buttons beeped and she pressed them in the preset sequence. Three short bleats signaled her success. She glanced down to where a slit of light from the hall crept into the unit. She could see his shadow.

Cara was about to call out to him. She wanted to chastise him for hovering, but his presence was disturbingly comforting. A childish part of her wanted to chase him off for that reason alone. She could accuse him of acting like a creeper. Say he was—

"Good night." His voice seeped through the door, quiet, calm and deep. "Try to rest tonight. Tomorrow is as good a day as any to start fresh."

She listened to his footsteps as he walked down the hall. The outer door latched with a loud *ka-thunk*. Stepping back into the unit, Cara placed her hands on her hips and let her head fall forward. She drew two breaths before releasing her hands and shaking her arms until they went noodle limp.

Once she'd released some of the tension in her neck and shoulders, she made her way into the small galley-style kitchen to sort through the bags Zarah had had delivered. As she unpacked each item, she made herself pause for a moment of gratitude.

She was alive.

She was well.

She had everything she needed.

Cara truly believed her life was better than a fairy tale. She got to build a company from the ground up with her two best friends at her side. Every day, she got to do work she loved. She brought people comfort in times of anxiety and solace in moments of sadness, and helped them find peace in the beats between each breath.

On the day Chris and Tom asked her to do the voice-over work on the new application they'd created as part of their final project before graduation, she'd planned to audition for a shampoo commercial. But they were desperate, and she didn't want to let them down. She'd been so naive when they met in their freshman dormitory at the University of California, Los Angeles. Like thousands of other transplants, she planned to be a star. Chris and Tom wanted to be the next Jobs and Wozniak.

They'd been the first friends she'd made in California, and for a lonesome girl from a small town in Arkansas, their friendship meant more than the possibility of commercial residuals.

She reached into another bag and her hand closed around a tube. She pulled it out and saw Zarah had thought to buy her favorite brand of deodorant. Tears filled her eyes as she offered up heartfelt gratitude for her young assistant.

Cara knew she had people who loved and supported her.

People who knew her and understood her better than her own family.

Her folks thought the whole acting thing was a phase. They didn't mind her going out to California for college because she'd sailed out on a flotilla of scholarships and financial aid programs. Cara knew they had not so secretly hoped when she got out to LA and realized how mercurial Hollywood could be, she'd settle into a more practical degree program. They hadn't counted on her loving every bit of the hustle and grind.

They never imagined she wouldn't come home and take over the land three generations of Becketts had toiled over. A sharp pang of guilt twanged through her as she glanced over at the phone she'd abandoned on the coffee table. Should she call them? Maybe not get into the details of what happened, but let them know she was coming to stay for a little while?

Her heart rate ramped up at the very thought, but the next thing she knew, she was palming the phone. Her thumb hovered over the keypad as she checked the time. They'd be getting ready for bed. Things had been strained between her and her parents for so long. They weren't estranged, exactly, but her refusal to come home after graduation had cracked the foundation of their relationship.

Biting her lip, she punched out a 424 area code rather than the 870 attached to the landline her parents insisted on keeping.

Zarah picked up on the second ring. "Hello?"

"It's me," Cara informed her.

Her assistant let out a long breath. "Are you okay?"

"Yes. Yes, I'm fine." Cara nodded, even though she knew the younger woman couldn't see her. Maybe she was trying to reassure herself.

"Did you get the stuff I ordered? Is the place okay?" the younger woman asked, breathless. "I can't believe this happened to you. In Arkansas! I mean, I expect to hear about bad stuff out here, but I didn't know you had anything more than, uh, farmland in Arkansas."

"You're not far off. Actually, rice is the biggest crop here," Cara said, doodling the words "rice is nice" on the first page of her new notebook.

Zarah's spongelike ability to absorb random bits of information was one of her most charming quirks. The quickest
way to talk her down was to load her up with tasty tidbits of
trivia she could whip out at a moment's notice.

"Really?" The younger woman hummed as she filed the
information away in her mind palace. "I had no idea."

"Facts are fun," Cara said, forcing a bright note into her
tone. "Were you able to get into my place without any trouble?"

"Oh, yeah. No problem. I grabbed your passport for ID
and found the credit card right where you said it would be. I
raided petty cash for a couple hundred and put it in the envelope in case. I overnighted it all to you in care of Special
Agent Dawson at the Arkansas State Police. It should arrive
before 8:00 a.m."

Cara fought the urge to roll her eyes. When Wyatt Dawson found out Zarah had sent supplies from one of the super-
stores to the condo, he insisted she call her assistant back
and route any future shipments through him. Cara thought
it was overkill, but she'd been too tired to fight him on it.

"Thank you so much for all you've done."

"Oh, jeez, no problem," Zarah said, allowing her native
Minnesotan to show through for a second. "I'm so relieved
you're okay. So scary, you know?"

Smiling her first genuine smile of the night, Cara said,
"I know."

"Are you calling me from the new phone?"

"Yes, but don't give the number to anyone yet. The police
are cloning my old number. Anything sent to it will show on
this one too. They're monitoring both numbers, so they can
capture any calls or texts."

"Oh. Cool." She gave a little laugh. "It sounds like they're
pretty cyber savvy there in Arkansas."

Cara frowned, both mildly offended on behalf of her home state and bemused by the younger woman's blunt assessment. "Yes, they are. But that also means the guy who has my phone might be checking it too, if he can get past my security code. I'm not putting anything past anyone these days."

"I totally hear you," Zarah said.

Tired, and not prepared to answer questions, Cara shifted into business mode. "Hey, so I need some contact information. If I send you a list, will you email them back to me?"

"Email? Can't I text them?"

Zarah sounded perplexed by the notion of using such antiquated means of communication. Smirking at the notebook where she started jotting names, Cara wondered if Zarah would find Special Agent Dawson nearly as cute if she passed on his suggestion regarding the pen and paper.

"We're trying to go low-tech on this," Cara informed her. "I'm staying off apps, and texts are not secure. We know my work email has been hacked, but I have an old address I use as a spam catcher. I was thinking maybe if you don't mind me sending a list to your personal email?"

"Oh! Yeah. Totally makes sense."

Zarah rattled off an email address. They ended the call and Cara tapped her pen against the pad as she racked her brain for any other contacts she wanted to add to her list. Then she opened the secure browser and attempted to access the email account she never used. It took three attempts before she recalled the correct password, and even then she had to run the gauntlet of selecting security images of cacti and bicycles before the server demanded access to send a one-time code to her phone.

Gnawing her bottom lip, she weighed the risk of exposure before typing in her digits. She figured her detractors would have to be pretty darn dedicated to watch her every move all the time. Besides, she'd done all of her travel correspondence through her work email. The odds of anyone tracking down the handle she'd barely used since college had to be slim.

She fired off the list of names along with her heartfelt thanks for going above and beyond, and the reassurance there was no hurry to reply because she'd be logging out and heading straight for the shower then bed. The message whooshed its way to California. Her inbox was full of unopened newsletters, discount codes and special offers she'd relegated to limbo. With a couple taps, she sent them all to the trash bin.

She logged out of the email server, then backed out of the secure browser, sure to wait until flames rolled up the screen as an indication the connection had been torched. Satisfied she'd done all she could to cover her tracks, she stowed the last of the food items before grabbing the clothes and toiletries and heading for the bathroom. The sooner she got to sleep, the sooner morning would come.

Standing under the hot spray, she did her level best to tap into the gratitude and positivity she touted on the app, but her mind continued to whirl. Then her ankles gave out.

Sitting on the floor of a strange tub with her legs drawn close and her head pressed to her knees, she let the tears flow. They ran down her cheeks hot and salty as the cooling water pummeled her shoulders and back. Shivering, she told herself everything would be better in the morning.

It had to be.

Because if things could get worse than being abducted at gunpoint, she didn't want to know how.

HEAVY POUNDING WOKE her from a fitful sleep. She wasn't quite ready to surface, but the dream of someone sawing her in half was every bit as disturbing as the persistent thumps.

Cracking an eyelid, Cara found herself staring at sunlight streaming through unfamiliar curtains. Another round of demanding knocks came, and the phone she'd clutched until she fell asleep buzzed insistently from under her pillow.

She sat up, her eyes gritty from too many tears and too little sleep.

Someone was calling her name through the door. She ran a hand over her hair. It was flat on one side and sticking up on the other. She'd fallen asleep while it was still damp.

"Cara? If you don't answer in the next thirty seconds, I'm busting down this door."

The person issuing the threat was a man. But it didn't sound like a threat. It sounded like a warning. Yanking the phone from its nesting spot, she swung her legs over the side of the bed as she read the name on the screen. Swiping with her thumb, she said, "Agent Dawson?"

"Why aren't you answering your door?" he demanded. His tone was edgy and sharp.

"I was sleeping," she grumbled, staggering across the living room to the door.

She started disengaging the locks, but his gravelly bark stopped her. "Peephole."

"I know it's you," she argued. "I can hear you through the door and the phone."

"Check anyway," he growled.

She obliged him with a huff. Sure enough, Special Agent Wyatt Dawson stood in the hall holding an overnight envelope and wearing a shearling-lined denim jacket. "Nice jacket," she said, matching him grump for grump. "You headed out to rope some steers this morning?"

"Disarm the alarm."

She wanted to tell him where he could get off, but she was

hoping the envelope contained the cash, cards and passport Zarah had shipped.

"Sir, yes, sir," she replied, turning away from the door. She disabled the alarm system, then twisted the locks. Stepping back to allow him entry, she muttered, "You're eager to get a jump on the day."

He stepped over the threshold, then quickly closed the door behind him. Once he had her locked in again, he turned and thrust the envelope at her. "Do you have a Webmail address?"

"What?"

"Do you have a Webmail email account?" he demanded.

"Yes, but I don't use—"

"Did you send an email to someone last night?"

Cara pushed her hand through her hair, her anger rising even as her stomach sank. "What if I did?" she challenged.

"If you did, you exposed your account and someone got hold of it," he shot back.

"How? I was barely on there for two minutes," she cried, incredulous.

"Doesn't take long if someone is tracking your every move. Did you do some kind of password recovery or two-step verification?"

She squeezed her eyes shut and blew out a long breath. Apparently, Wyatt Dawson knew a confession when he heard one, because he pressed on.

"We got a call from a sergeant with Company E this morning. A woman claiming to be Elizabeth Beckett contacted them about an email she received concerning her daughter," he said, watching her closely.

"Elizabeth Beckett? My mom?"

His lips flattened into a thin line. "I suppose so." Wyatt pulled out his phone and started tapping. Once he got what he was after, he turned his phone over to her. It was a photo of a computer screen. On the screen was an email from the account she'd used to contact Zarah the night before, but this one was addressed to her parents' email address.

It was a ransom letter from a man who claimed to have taken her from the parking deck at Clinton National Airport in Little Rock. The amount he was asking for to secure her release was absurd. Her parents were ranchers. Even if they sold every head of cattle and every acre of land, they couldn't have come up with the outrageous figure demanded.

She looked at the time stamp on the email. It was sent less than an hour after she emailed Zarah the list of contact names. "Oh, my God," she whispered. She swiped at the phone screen, desperate to make the message disappear. "I need to call them."

"They know you're okay," Wyatt assured her, gently removing his phone from her grasp. "I spoke to your mother. Your father too. I gave them a brief rundown on what's happening, but I think we should vacate in case this location is compromised."

"Compromised?" she repeated, willing her brain to catch up.

"They obviously have a thumb on your correspondence. Probably phished your work email to identify your personal accounts. I'm going to need details on everything since you were first aware someone had your information." He blew out a breath, his hands braced on his hips as he scanned the condo. "Gather your stuff. You can call your folks once we're out of here."

Her stuff? She looked down at the package he'd thrust at her. Pulling the tear strip, she peered into the envelope. An envelope she assumed held the cash Zarah had mentioned, two credit cards—though who knew if they'd be any good to her—and her passport.

"What do you mean *we*?"

"Apparently, Mrs. Elizabeth Beckett knows people," he said with a wry smile. "You related to Paul Stanton? An uncle or something?"

"Paul Stanton?" she repeated blankly. "I, uh, I don't have an uncle. There's my aunt CeCe, but she never married."

"Nope. The name doesn't ring any bells? Lieutenant Governor Paul Stanton," he repeated.

She squeezed her eyes shut as she tried to recall the bits and pieces of hometown news her mother relayed whenever they spoke. Finally, the light bulb came on. "Oh, Paul Stanton. He's not actually my uncle. A family friend. Or friend of my mother's, I should say. He and my mom went to prom together and kept in touch. My dad hates him, but I remember her telling me he's some kind of big shot now."

"Well, your mama called him, and good old Uncle Paul made a couple calls, and it looks like you've got yourself your very own special agent," he said, holding his arms out wide.

"What?"

"Come on." He made his way to the kitchen and began bagging the supplies she'd unpacked the night before. When she didn't move, he motioned to the bedroom. "I'll fill you in on the way."

"On the way to where?" she asked, standing her ground.

He dropped a box of her favorite cheese crackers into the delivery bag and looked up at her, one dark brow raised. "I am to escort you home, Ms. Beckett."

"Home?" Dread pooled in the pit of her stomach when she pictured poor Nancy bandaged up in her hospital bed. "To California?"

"Oh, no, ma'am. I'm under strict instruction to deliver you into the hands of Mrs. Elizabeth Beckett ASAP."

"My mama?"

He looked her straight in the eye. "We're headin' to Snowball. Hope you have a jacket. It can be chilly up in the hills this time of year."

Chapter Four

Forty-five minutes later, he had Cara Beckett and her meager belongings packed into a state-issued SUV heading north on US 65. They were quiet as they exited the busy metro area north of Conway and headed up into the foothills of the Ozark Mountains. The moment she'd sat down in the car, she called her mother from his phone, having surrendered the new mobile to him by way of tossing it at the condo's sofa.

Wyatt didn't call her out on her decidedly less-than-Zen attitude. Her life had been ripped out from under her feet in the past week or so. And with the LYYF company's public offering about to take off, things were only going to get more hectic.

He'd offered her coffee and a fast-food breakfast, but she'd refused, keeping her arms crossed tight over her chest. He ordered a bottle of water along with his morning dose of caffeine.

Caught by a red light in Greenbrier, Wyatt cast a sidelong glance at his passenger. She sat stoically staring through the windshield when he offered her the bottle of water. "Single-use containers are poisoning our air and killing our oceans," she said stiffly.

He stared back at her, keeping his expression neutral though he could feel his ears heating. "How did you sleep last night?"

"I didn't," she retorted.

He waggled the evil water bottle in front of her. "A lack of proper rest can lead to dehydration. Right now, my mission is to keep you alive. We'll worry about the planet tomorrow."

"Exactly the sort of attitude responsible for our current climate change crisis."

"I'm not covering the planet today. I'm tasked with taking care of you. Drink the water," he ordered, tossing the bottle into her lap as the light changed.

He accelerated, trying to swallow back his exasperation. She wasn't sulking, per se, but she was not thrilled about the arrangement. And she wasn't drinking the water. He added stubborn to his mental list of things he knew about Cara Beckett. A list not nearly long enough if he was going to be any help in figuring out who was behind the cyber and real-world attacks against her.

"So, you grew up in Snowball?"

She shook her head. "Snowball is the closest dot on the map."

"Your parents own a ranch?"

"A little over six hundred acres. My dad keeps anywhere between fifty and seventy-five head of Black Angus cattle."

Her tone was flat, but he picked up a hint of pride in her delivery. "Wow. Sounds like a lot. Is it a lot?" he asked, glancing over at her for confirmation.

She shrugged. "I'd say about average for a family ranch." Her monotone response faded into a faintly mocking tone. "Let me guess, you're a city boy? Grew up in Little Rock?"

He shook his head, his lips twitching into a smirk meant to show her exactly how wrong she was about him. "Nope. Born and raised in Stuttgart, home of Ricebirds."

He felt her appraising stare. "Were you a farm kid?"

Unable to keep up the ruse, he allowed the smirk to take over as he shook his head. "Nah. My dad sold insurance."

"Ah."

Awkward silence descended like a thick fog. Grasping for information and a conversational straw, he asked, "You get along with your parents?"

She shot him a sidelong glance. "Do you?"

"Yeah," he replied without hesitation.

"I do too, but you know what they say…"

"What?"

This time, she couldn't repress the smile. "You think you're enlightened, spend a week with your family."

He chuckled. "I get you."

They drove in silence for a while. Finally, he prompted her to tell him her version of the story. "Start at the beginning. What was the first odd thing you noticed?"

Cara's fingers curled around the edge of the console between them. She was quiet, and for a minute, he thought perhaps she would not answer. He couldn't blame her for wanting to play things close to the chest. Her personal information had been scattered across multiple forums. He'd seen at least a half-dozen entries himself. And the threats came standard with this kind of cyberattack. People talked tough when tucked safely behind a keyboard. But somebody, or some people, had taken a giant step out of the shadow of internet anonymity.

Hopefully, it would make them easier to find.

"It's hard to say," she murmured, her face turned toward the scenery whizzing past.

The fall foliage was near peak color as October gave way to November. It seemed wrong to spoil such beautiful scenery with talk of ugliness.

"There have always been messages. Even before the app

took off. You know, the usual online slime. People trying to slide into my inbox. Once LYYF started gaining traction, I got hit up for money more often than I was hit on," she said, a wry smile twisting her lips. "Tom likes to say he knew we'd made it when guys starting fishing for my account numbers rather than my phone number."

"Tom is Tom Wasinski," he clarified, shooting her a glance.

"Yes. Tom Wasinski."

"He and Chris Sharpe are your partners in LYYF," he stated.

"Yes."

"And you knew them from…college," he prompted, hoping to get her talking.

"Yes. We were suite mates our freshman year. Stayed friends through school and after."

"You did the voice-over work for them from the beginning?"

When she didn't add anything more to the story, he stole a peek at her. She stared stone-faced through the windshield, and he winced. "Sorry. I didn't mean to trample all over your story."

"Not my story," she said in a clipped tone. "But you seem pretty well-versed in the lore of LYYF, so who am I to spoil it for you?"

Biting the inside of his cheek to keep from groaning his frustration with himself, Wyatt tightened his grip on the steering wheel. "You're right. I'm sorry. I think I was trying to impress you with how much I know." He offered her a wan smile as they slowed to pass through one of the myriad small towns along the route. "I want you to feel comfortable talking to me. Safe. I'm here to help."

She shifted in her seat, turning to face him more fully. "If you want me to feel comfortable telling my story, you might try listening. I don't need you to recite the press clippings to me."

Chastened, he ducked his head to acknowledge the point scored. "I'm sorry," he repeated. The tires hummed as silence overtook them once again. He waited, but when she didn't volunteer anything more, he pressed his lips together and nodded, owning his ignorance. "Would you tell me what happened?"

She blew out a long breath, letting her head fall back against the seat. The woman beside him didn't look anything like the glossy, glowing guru on his app. She looked haunted. Hunted. When she spoke, her voice was hoarse.

"Everyone latches on to the voice work like all I did was show up and read a few cue cards one day."

For once in his life, he had sense enough to keep his lips zipped.

"They were working on a finance app." She gave a dry little laugh. "It wasn't much more than a bookkeeping tool. Like one of those account trackers my mom used to use to record each check or ATM withdrawal. You know, the little booklet with three years' worth of calendars printed on there?"

"Checkbook register," he said with a nod.

"Exactly. Anyway, they were developing it all through school. It changed and evolved as we did. People weren't tracking checks and more banks had apps where you could see your transactions real-time, so they started retooling it to be more of a finance guide for kids our age." She waved a hand dismissively. "Simple stuff. Interest calculators, a stock market widget and some how-to guides one of the business majors a couple years older than us wrote up as part of their thesis project."

"Interesting."

She scoffed. "It wasn't. It was boring. But by the time we

graduated, almost everyone we knew had made some sort of contribution." She gave him a smirk. "I recorded a few videos with tips and tricks for acing job interviews."

"And this was under the LYYF banner?"

"At the time it was Life. *L-I-F-E*. We even had some cheesy tagline about it being the only tool a person needed to win at the game of life."

"Catchy."

"Anyhow, the concept grew and evolved, and as Tom and Chris became better programmers, the possibilities kept expanding."

She propped her elbow on the door and pressed her thumb into her temple as if talking about the past gave her a headache. But he didn't give her an out. He couldn't. Her life was on the line.

"How did LYYF as we know it come about?"

She gazed out at the passing scenery. "Sometime in my sophomore year, I'd gone on a commercial audition where I met a woman who was into Transcendental Meditation. We got to talking, she told me about a retreat happening near campus. It was free, I was…searching…"

The last word trailed away, and he let it go for a few minutes. He knew sifting through memories was sometimes like reading lines of data—whatever you were looking for usually popped out the moment you let your focus go a bit fuzzy.

They were navigating one of the steep downhill stretches before she spoke again.

"Anyhow. I got into meditation and yoga as a way to deal with the constant rejection," she said quietly.

"And all this time you were in school?"

She nodded. "I booked a few local ads, but never a national campaign. I was too generic for most casting directors."

He blinked, taken aback. The woman had to know she

was a knockout, but her unflinchingly harsh assessment of her looks sounded too clinical to be false modesty.

"You're hardly a generic anything."

The words he intended as a compliment came out awkward, stilted by his desire not to cross any professional boundaries. When he chanced a peek at her, he found her wearing the serene half smile she wore on the app's welcome screen.

"Not only is he a protector, but also he's a poet," she mocked, eyes crinkling with humor.

Heat prickled his neck. Determined to brazen out his embarrassment, he shot her a quelling look. "You know what I mean."

"I do. And thank you," she said, sounding thoroughly amused. "But pretty enough by Arkansas standards means I wasn't even in the ballpark in LA." Before he could argue the point further, she continued. "I was telling Tom all about this breathing technique I was using to help deal with nerves, and he said something about how it wasn't only actors who needed coping skills. The next thing I knew, I was cooking up a short script about how I got into meditation and the practical applications." She shrugged. "We purposefully omitted as much of the new-age terminology as possible and replaced it with some of the corporate catchphrases we were hearing all around us. Soon, we had about ten sessions written up, each focusing on a particular stressor or coping technique we thought would be helpful. I recorded them on my phone sitting in my closet using an earphone mic. And now you know the real LYYF origin story."

"Why were you sitting in a closet?" he asked, perplexed by this odd little detail.

"Sound absorption," she explained. "It had this nasty beige carpet left over from the nineties. We hung blankets on the walls and pushed most of the clothes back so they wouldn't be too close around me, but yeah. It worked."

"I guess so," he said, impressed.

"By the time we graduated, the guys were off and running with the life management idea. I was still making the rounds, doing auditions and waiting tables."

"Where were they getting their money?"

"Chris had money. Trust fund kid. Tom's parents supported him too. His dad was a surgeon and did well enough, but it wasn't inherited money like the Sharpes'. But Tom's parents were the competitive type. They wanted to keep up with the Sharpes, so they pretty much gave him an unlimited line of credit."

"And your folks…" he trailed off.

"Are rich in land and not much more. You know how it is," she said with a shrug.

And he did. There were plenty of families like hers around Stuttgart. Rice farmers with large stretches of valuable farmland who scrimped, saved and relied on government subsidies to keep from selling parcels off as the modern world closed in around them.

Cara continued her story. "When those first ten sessions started getting more clicks than some of the other sessions, they asked if I wanted to do more." She shrugged. "I wrote another ten and people seemed to like those too."

"And eventually, they asked if you wanted to be their partner?"

Pressing the tip of her tongue to her upper lip, she shook her head hard. "Uh, no," she said with a sharp little laugh. "They asked me to write and record more. I had two waitressing jobs, was pulling some temp hours doing reception work and still trying to land a part, any part. I told them I didn't have time."

"I see."

"A couple weeks passed, then Chris called me back saying they would pay me."

"Did they?"

She nodded. "A thousand bucks for another ten sessions. It doesn't sound like much now, and in context, but at the time it was the difference between making rent or buying a plane ticket home." She sighed, twisting her fingers together in her lap. "But, naturally, they were always more focused on the technology than the content. When the new sessions dropped and users started asking for more, they didn't want to spend time and money on developing content to be delivered regularly. Chris was the one who suggested they cut me in as a partner."

"Sounds like a big leap. For all of you," he added.

"It was a great deal for them. Particularly if the app didn't find traction. I was responsible for writing, producing and performing all consumer-facing wellness and lifestyle content. Research, scripting, recording…everything. We used to like to joke about how they made the widgets, I made the rest."

He let out a low whistle. "I had no idea."

"Most people don't." She gave a short laugh. "At the time, I was still auditioning for my big Hollywood career, so I was happy to let them handle what little press we got for LYYF. Since the only exposure we got in the early days was on tech blogs and forums, the narrative developed from there."

"Chris and Tom went on to become tech stars and you were cast as the wannabe actress who finagled her way into a very lucrative partnership."

She nodded, but her smile was self-deprecating. "I can't complain. It's been the most celebrated role of my entire acting career."

"Made you famous."

"It made me known in certain circles," she corrected. "Anyway, my point is, there have always been people who believed I didn't deserve what I had. They let their feelings be known on forums and chat rooms, then when the app itself became geared more toward interaction, direct messages. So, you see, it's hard to pinpoint a time when the harassment started, because it's been happening all along."

Wyatt hummed his understanding. The tech world was still disproportionately male, and some quarters were openly hostile to female interlopers. "What was your first hint it was going beyond the usual?"

"I started getting more direct messages on the app and on social media."

"What kind of DMs?"

"The usual. Name-calling. People saying I'm nothing but a parasite. No talent. Ugly. Commentary on my body, my voice, the way I breathe," she said tiredly.

"The way you breathe is a lifesaver for some people." The words were out of his mouth before he could vet them. Mortified, he kept his gaze locked on the series of curves ahead of them.

"I tell myself it is," she said quietly. "But some days it's easier to believe the bad over the good."

He knew the feeling too well. "I understand."

"I didn't start to get worried until the texts began."

"I imagine those were more of the same?"

"Yes," she confirmed. "But coming directly to my phone, they felt more…menacing."

"What did you do?"

"I sent them to Tom. He's always up for solving a mystery. In this case it wasn't much of a challenge for him. A simple search showed my name popping up in various forums. The next thing I knew, we found my cell number along with my home address, as well as several personal email addresses posted." He sensed her looking at him and turned. "The one I used last night was not one of them."

"So someone is actively monitoring your internet usage," he concluded, meeting her gaze.

She heaved a weary sigh as she smoothed her eyebrows with her thumb and middle finger. "I need to text Zarah and tell her I've checked out of the rental."

He nodded. "Use my phone." As if on cue, his phone rang. The display showed the caller to be Trooper Masterson. He hesitated for a moment before answering, but at Cara's questioning look, accepted the call.

"This is Dawson. We're hands-free," he announced, wanting to give the other man fair warning.

"Dawson. Is Ms. Beckett with you?" Masterson asked.

"Yes," Wyatt said.

"I'm here," Cara answered at the same time.

"Ms. Beckett, I wanted to let you know your rental car has been recovered," the trooper informed her.

"It has?"

"Where?" Wyatt asked, stepping over her words in turn.

"It was found in section 104 of the parking deck at the airport," the older man replied.

"Section 104," Cara murmured.

"Anything recovered?" Wyatt pressed.

"We have a team going over it now, but it appears most of your belongings were left intact. There was a large leather bag with your wallet, phone and other personal items on the front floorboard, and a travel bag in the back seat."

He let off the gas and coasted toward the shoulder of the road, tires crunching on loose gravel as he slowed to a stop. A car whizzed past. Seconds passed before a speeding tanker truck left them rocking in its wake. He and Cara shared a glance.

"Any cash or credit cards in the wallet?" Wyatt asked.

"My officer on scene checked. Says it doesn't look like your passenger took anything."

Wyatt did his best to keep his expression impassive. She was searching his face for clues, and he didn't have one to give. "So no theft," he said, his tone flat.

"Other than the vehicle," Masterson supplied.

"Which was found in the exact spot where Ms. Beckett found it," Wyatt supplied.

"But I… He…" she spluttered. "This wasn't some fantasy abduction I made up to scare people," she insisted, voice rising in agitation. "The truck driver. Eustace. Mr. Stubbs. He saw us. He saw me jump out of the car. He saw a man take off with the rental car."

"We do have Mr. Stubbs, the driver who picked you up. He gave a statement and as much of a description as he could," Masterson said in a patronizingly soothing tone. "And we may get lucky with some hair or other fibers."

But it didn't sound like he was expecting much. And even if they did come up with forensic evidence, the perpetrator would have to be somewhere in the system for there to be a match.

"Okay," Wyatt said, hoping to redirect the conversation. "Let me know what the forensics team finds. I have Emma Parker with the CCD working on some data tracking for us too. I'll have her loop you in if she uncovers anything helpful to the case."

"Appreciate it," Masterson said gruffly. "I'll keep you updated."

Wyatt thanked the man, then ended the call.

A logging truck rumbled past. Two minivans and an SUV

zipped along close behind it. All three of the drivers jockeyed to be in position to overtake the larger vehicle, all too aware once they got past Clinton and started climbing into the hills, the highway would narrow to a single lane in each direction. When they hit the switchbacks, there would only be the occasional passing lane made available for traffic relief. He'd be stuck behind them all.

He was already so far behind.

Who was hacking into Cara Beckett's accounts? Who disliked a woman who swore by gratitude journals and daily meditation enough to terrorize her? Chase her from her home? Kidnap her in broad daylight?

"Why would he leave everything?"

Her tremulous question broke into his thoughts. He turned to face her, but when his eyes met hers, he could see she already knew the answer. Robbery was never the intent.

This time, she spoke in little more than a whisper. "Why does someone want to hurt me?"

"I don't know," he answered honestly. "But I promise I'm going to do my best to figure out who it is and stop them."

Understanding arced like an electric current between them. But she didn't reach for his phone. Instead, she held his gaze so long he had to jerk his attention back to the road.

"Do you mind if we stop and get a coffee before we head for my parents' house?" she asked. "I'd like a moment to… collect my thoughts."

Wyatt nodded and checked their location against the GPS. "I know exactly the place." Hitting his blinker, he craned his neck to check traffic. A rooster tail of grit and dust rose behind them as he steered the SUV back onto the highway.

Chapter Five

Cara clutched the paper cup holding her coffee close as a breeze with a biting edge to it whipped her hair from her forehead. The view from the scenic overlook touted on a billboard outside of Marshall did not disappoint. The valley stretched below them like a patchwork quilt sewn from scraps of vibrant autumn colors. Red, orange and gold specimens shone bright against a backdrop of dark evergreens and leaves already dried to crisp golden brown.

"The cemetery where my mother's grandparents are buried sits on top of a hill covered in these huge red maple trees," she murmured when Wyatt approached. "Every fall, they turn the most incredible red-gold color I've ever seen. I bet it's spectacular about now."

"We can go there if you like. It's not like we'll have to hide out in your parents' basement."

"Good to hear," she said. He half turned and flashed a wry smile. "Because they don't have a basement. Nothing but a nasty old storm cellar filled with ancient canning jars and spiders." She glanced back at the SUV where he'd been making and taking calls while she ruminated. "Anything new?"

"We have an IP address from where the email was sent. It gave us a trail to follow. There's a forum user from Hot Springs we suspect may have been your, uh, passenger."

Cara whirled to face him. She swiped at her hair ineffectually. "Is it so easy to find people?"

"If you know how and where to look. Special Agent Parker has a talent for tracking these things down. Probably because when she was younger, she used the same talent to cover her own tracks."

"What do you mean?"

He smirked. "A member of our team was once a teenage hacker."

"Like Tom." The words slipped past her lips. She raised her hand to cover her mouth, but it was too late. She could tell by his expression he'd caught them. When he didn't express any surprise or press her for additional information, her eyes narrowed. "Did you know?"

He shrugged. "It's one of those open secret things. The truth is, a lot of people who go into programming or security started out trying to break into things. It's not much different from kids who grow up to be mechanics or engineers taking stuff apart to see how it's put back together again."

"Except it's illegal."

"Right. But most don't do anything truly harmful like hack into NORAD."

She blinked twice. "Right," she echoed. Then, shaking her head in disbelief, she turned back to the view. She cradled her coffee in the crook of her arm and pulled the cuffs of her sweater down over her hands. "So, they're looking into this lead?"

He nodded. "She'll call me as soon as they can get something solid."

She drew on her bottom lip, biting down to quell the swirl of anxiety and anticipation pooling in her belly. Letting her gaze go soft and unfocused, she imagined pulling the lovely patchwork blanket of fall foliage up around her shoulders.

The visualization helped a little but not enough. She needed to let Wyatt know what he was in for on this trip.

"You should know my parents and I have a…shaky relationship."

She felt his glance but could tell by the shift in his posture he'd gone back to staring out over the vista. "Okay."

"We don't fight or anything," she felt compelled to add, waving her coffee cup in a dismissive circle. "I'm an only child and let's say we wanted different things—for me—and leave it there."

"I understand."

He shifted his weight, and Cara got the feeling he actually did.

"My dad wanted me to take over his insurance agency. They only had me and my older sister. Shelby went off to school at Ole Miss, met my brother-in-law there and never came home. When I was up at the U of A, I majored in computer science. I told my dad I could use everything I learned to bring the agency up to date, automate everything, you know…"

When he let the story trail off, she turned to face him again. "But you never went to work for him."

Wyatt shook his head. "I met a guy who worked for the Department of Public Safety. They were recruiting on campus. Looking for people with tech skills to join the state police. I imagined myself as the guy who figured out who was sneaking around the dark web and what they were doing and stopped it all before things got too out of hand," he said dryly.

"So you and Agent…Parker, was it?" He nodded. "You come at things from different angles."

He shrugged, his hands buried deep in the pockets of his jeans. "I suppose you can say we do. But we work well together. Balance each other out."

"That's nice. Balance is good." She sighed. "I suppose we should get moving." Turning on her heel, she walked off in the direction of the car. She settled her coffee into the cup holder and waited for Wyatt to join her.

He took another moment to drink in the view. Which gave her the same opportunity with him. He was tall by Hollywood standards, probably just over six foot. He was lean, but not skinny. The Henley he wore with his jeans showed off broad shoulders and toned arms, but he didn't appear to be pumped up like a gym rat. All in all, he suited the scenery. Natural and unaffected.

He dropped into the seat with a soft "Oof," and she jumped.

"Sorry," she said, laughing at her own skittishness.

"No worries," he assured her.

"I just need to take a breath," she murmured. When she inhaled deeply, he did the same.

"Okay, now let it go," he said, parroting the words she used so often in her meditations as he started the car. "Now breathe in. Breathe in LYYF."

His eyes crinkled as he said the last bit, and a laugh burbled out of her. She reached over and gave his arm a friendly swat. "Don't mock me."

"Mock you?" he repeated through a laugh. "You? The guru? Never."

They'd strapped into their seats when the phone she'd left in the console vibrated. Beside her, Wyatt tensed. They both eyed the device warily.

"Text message," he grumbled, giving the notification the stink eye. "Know the number?"

She shrugged. "Not off the top of my head, but I don't memorize many numbers anymore."

"We've been forwarding all calls from unknown numbers

to headquarters. You should only be getting messages from people who have the new number."

"I gave it to Zarah. She may have passed it along to Tom or Chris," she speculated.

He nodded, but neither of them reached for the phone despite another insistent buzz.

"I suppose you should check it," he said at last.

A chill of apprehension ran down her spine as she leaned over to grab the phone. The screen sprang to life, and Cara sucked in a sharp breath when she saw the number in the little red circle. Seven. Someone had sent seven text messages to her phone. She opened the first.

856-784-4544: Have you missed us, Cara?

773-238-5795: Did you think we wouldn't be able to tell you rerouted us?

413-648-7993: I don't think she wants to talk to us anymore. I'm hurt.

630-721-9173: Hear she's run away to Arkansas, of all places.

325-545-1899: Arkansas sounds…like Arkansas. I bet Cara has ditched her shoes, cut off her jeans, and is kissin' a cousin right now.

213-566-5487: I can't believe some hick from a flyover state thinks she can cash in on Chris and Tom's genius because she slept with one or both of them back in the day. Where is Arkansas, anyway?

565-982-1167: You breathing LYYF in, Cara? Does the air taste better in Ar-Kansas?

"Oh, my God," she whispered.

"What?" Wyatt leaned over to get a look at the screen.

"They're texting this number," she said, jerking her gaze up to meet his.

"What?"

"They know we were forwarding calls and messages," she said, eyes wide. "They must have somehow traced the forwarding back to this number."

The phone in her hand vibrated again, and she jerked so violently she squeezed it from her grip. Bobbling the device, she let out a gusty whoosh of breath when Wyatt caught and held it still in his steady hand. Then, Cara read the latest entry.

228-798-1163: It's nice here, isn't it, Cara. Warm days and cool nights. Isn't sweater weather the best?

She began to shake. "Oh, no," she murmured, shaking her head. It started out a slow denial but grew more adamant with each swing. "No. No. No. They can't come here." She turned pleading eyes on Wyatt, unable to hide behind a mask of cool any longer. "We can't go to my parents' house."

"We're going to your parents' house," he replied, pressing the button to power down the phone.

"But we can't. I can't." Her voice grew sharper with agitation. "I can't bring all this to their doorstep. They didn't want me to be a part of this from the very start. I can't show up with a passel of stalkers hot on my tail."

"Understood," he said in an annoyingly calm tone. "But there isn't a passel of stalkers following you."

"Didn't you read what they said? It is sweater weather. They know where we are going."

"They do not. Those texts were all sent through an auto-dialer. The phone numbers were too random. Someone may know you flew into Little Rock, and they may figure you know people here, but it doesn't mean they know where you were heading."

"They emailed my mother a ransom demand," she practically shouted at him.

"Because they found someone with the name Beckett in your address book on an ancient email account," he countered. "They got lucky."

"No one gets that lucky," she argued.

"Either way, it doesn't matter. When I spoke to your mother, she said the first thing she did was pick up the phone and call her friend the lieutenant governor's office. From a landline," he added. "She didn't reply to the email or forward it to anyone from her account."

"Paul Stanton," was all she could manage to mutter.

"Your mother didn't do anything but open the message. They have no way of knowing they hit a bull's-eye."

He tossed the phone back into the console. Cara wanted to snatch it back and toss it out the window. But she knew she couldn't. They would need every scrap of evidence they could gather.

He swiveled in his seat to look her straight in the eye. "All the sender could possibly know is someone opened it. They're fishing, Cara," he said, reaching over and wrapping his fingers around her forearm. "I wouldn't take you anywhere near there if I didn't believe we could keep you all safe."

The gesture surprised her. From the moment they'd met, he'd kept a respectable distance between them. But this touch didn't feel like a boundary crossed. The size of his hand was reassuring. The warmth of it, a balm. He held her gaze, sure and steady. And she believed him. He would do as he said. He'd keep her safe.

"Fishing," she repeated.

"Or phishing, with a *p-h*, if you would," he said with a self-deprecating smirk. "Don't freak out, Cara. We're on top of this, you have my word."

"I don't know you. Your word may not be good for much," she muttered sourly.

One side of his mouth kicked up. "Let me put it this way. I value my career too much to take a celebrity who has been the victim of a crime, and has friends in high places, into a situation I believe to be dangerous to her or the people around her."

She choked on a laugh. "Celebrity? Hardly. And my mother is the one with the friends in high places. I haven't lived here since I was eighteen. I doubt I could pick the actual governor out of a lineup, much less the guy my mom went to the Marshall High prom with in 1978."

"I guess we should consider you an unreliable witness, then," he teased, reversing out of the parking spot. "For all we know, good old Uncle Paul Stanton might have been the one tryin' to hitch a ride with you at the airport."

"Ha ha."

He glanced over at her before accelerating onto the highway again. "I wouldn't put you or your parents in danger. I don't want to be in danger," he added with a laugh. "I know the title special agent sounds cool and all, but I'm a desk jockey. A computer nerd, remember?"

She huffed a laugh. "I've spent most of my adult life surrounded by computer nerds. Trust me, you carry the special agent thing off much better."

His lips curved into a sly smile. "I think there may have been a compliment wrapped up in there somewhere."

"Only an observation," she disputed, willing herself not to blush. Focusing on the curving road winding its way down into the valley carved by the Buffalo National River, she steered the conversation back to the investigation. "Tell me what's happening behind the scenes. Maybe I'll feel better about everything if I know what's going on behind the curtain."

Wyatt nodded. "I get you." He paused. His mouth puckered as he considered his words. "Okay, so we start with what we know. Someone has hacked into your accounts. They likely found their way in through one of your personal accounts rather than something attached to LYYF. Corporate security, particularly in tech firms, tends to be tight. Corporate espionage and so forth."

"I think everyone at LYYF knows I'm not the one who will be swiping critical codes," she said dryly.

"Perhaps not, but I'd wager most people inside and outside the company would assume you have access to critical information."

He lifted his foot off the gas and signaled for the left turn onto AR-74. Leaving the highway behind, they crossed Bear Creek and headed deep into the rolling hills and lush valleys of Searcy County.

"I'm guessing it was through a social media platform. They tend to be the most vulnerable, and some barely even try to make it hard to cage user information. From there, they likely gained access to other platforms, and possibly your company accounts." He paused for a moment, mulling something over. "Did you receive emails at your LYYF address as well as your personal accounts?"

"Yes, but they started with PicturSpam messages. I think you're right, they messaged on various other accounts, including LYYF, before the emails started."

"And I assume you were getting direct messages and

emails long before they leaked your information and the texts started."

"I wouldn't say long before," she hedged.

"In internet terms, long can mean hours or days," he clarified. "Think wildfire speed."

The Californian in her shuddered at the comparison, but she nodded. "Right. It was probably no more than a day or so. It seemed like everything happened at once."

"I can take a good guess at what most of the messages said, but tell me someone said something to make you hop on a plane less than two weeks before your company goes public and you become a multimillionaire."

Cara stared out at the scenery, wishing she could jump out and hide behind one of the huge round bales of hay dotting an autumn-browned pasture. Heck, it wouldn't be the first time she'd leaped from a vehicle this week. But Wyatt was sailing down the county highway at a steady clip, and she knew there was no way she could outrun the madness infiltrating her life. The only way out would be through, she reminded herself sternly.

"It wasn't what they said, it was what they did," she said, unable to look directly at him.

"Okay," he replied, the very soul of patience. "What did they do?"

"Well, let's see…" Pausing to gulp down the fear clawing at her throat, she focused on her hands clasped in her lap. "There was the petty vandalism. Nasty words spray-painted on my garage door, crude graffiti on my driveway. I've gone through three mailboxes in two weeks. All this in addition to the barrage of written and verbal harassment."

"Death threats?"

He asked the question as casually as if he was curious about her favorite color. So she answered in the same offhanded way. "Of course. Who gets doxed and doesn't get their fair share of death threats?"

Wyatt cast a quelling look in her direction. "Any the police were particularly interested in?"

"I'd like to believe they found all of them interesting, but there were a couple with, uh, specifics."

"You gonna tell me, or do I need to wait until the records we requested from California come through?"

She drew a deep breath, then let it out to the count of six. "One…person…said they liked my dog, and they'd be sure to take good care of it when I died."

He glanced over at her, his brow knit. "Your dog? I thought you said you have a cat."

"Half a cat," she corrected. "JuJu is a time-share."

"A stray you and the neighbor both feed," he recalled.

"My neighbor had a dog, though. Has. She has a dog. They are both alive and well, thank God."

Wyatt shifted in his seat, and she knew he was catching on, but she wasn't quite ready to say more. Instead, she pointed to a large metal building ahead of them. "Go past the Bakers' barn, you'll want to take a right on County Road 36. The road is barely more than one lane, and Mr. Baker likes to make a point out of farm equipment having the right of way around here, so look out for cranky old men on tractors."

"Got it."

Wyatt flipped on the turn signal even though there was no other car in sight. Cara smiled. He must have been telling the truth about growing up in farm country. Only city dwellers waited until the last second to signal their intention to turn. Out in the country, one never knew who or what might be coming up behind or poking along around a bend.

The tires scrambled for purchase on the crumbling concrete roadbed. Cara was pleased to note he'd heeded her caution and accelerated at a sedate pace. He let a good mile or so pass before he asked, "What happened to your neighbor?"

"She was out walking her dog. A car pulled up and a guy jumped out and grabbed her. He had a knife," she said, her words ending in a whisper.

"He stabbed her?"

Knowing he was watching her out of the corner of his eye, she simply nodded.

"But she wasn't fatally wounded," he confirmed.

"No."

"And the dog wasn't hurt."

Cara couldn't help but release a tense little laugh. He sounded so falsely encouraging it was ridiculous. She didn't know Wyatt Dawson well at all, but she felt safe in assuming optimism didn't come naturally to him. Why would it? He was a cop. He spent his days up to his elbows in all the worst things people did to one another.

"Buster is fine. Has a new little harness with LAPD printed on the back." She nodded to a crossroad ahead of them. "Keep going, but our turn will be coming up on the left."

"Got it. So Buster is an official K-9 officer now?"

"I wouldn't say official, but he was tough enough to get one of the officers to say every department should train a pack of Pomeranians. They may not be able to take a bad guy down, but they can sure wake the neighborhood." She pointed to a narrow driveway marked with three blue reflectors on their left. "Here we are. Home sweet home."

Chapter Six

When they pulled to a stop in front of the single-story ranch house at the end of a very long lane, a lazy yellow Labrador retriever bestirred itself enough to let out a single warning bark, then lay back down. Apparently, he felt he said enough. No one would ever accuse the big yellow dog of being a Pomeranian.

Wyatt barely switched off the engine before a tall, slender woman with long gray-blond hair woven into a thick braid burst through the screen door and bounded down the stairs.

"You're here," she cried, arms flung wide.

Cara fell out of the passenger seat and into the woman's embrace. "We're here," she replied, her voice muffled by an exuberant hug.

Wyatt watched them, arrested by the sight of the two women wound tight around one another. He nearly laughed out loud when he spotted a man wearing a shearling-lined denim jacket just like his and an Arkansas Razorbacks ball cap speeding toward them on an all-terrain utility vehicle. Her father abandoned the battered old gator before it came to a complete stop and hopped the low fence separating yard from pasture.

Wyatt noted the older couple were both strikingly attractive. Looking at them, it was no stretch to see into Cara's future.

"Hey, there," Cara's father said gruffly, pulling his daughter from her mother's arms and into his own. Like his wife and daughter, he was tall, but James Beckett was anything but willowy. Barrel-chested and burly, the man was more akin to a sprawling live oak tree.

"Hi, Daddy," she murmured as he crushed her to him.

"Hi, Sugar," her father grumbled into the top of her head. Without releasing his hold on Cara, he extended a hand toward Wyatt. "You're with the state police?"

"Yes, sir. Wyatt Dawson." He supplied his name as he shook the man's hand.

"I'm Betsy and this is Jim, and in case you haven't figured it out, we're Cara's mama and daddy."

"I put the pieces together," he said as he shook hands with Elizabeth. "Pleased to meet you both. Wish it were under better circumstances."

"Oh, my stars, I know." Elizabeth Beckett threaded her hand through his arm and propelled him in the direction of the porch. "I can't even believe this is happening." She whirled and pinned Cara with an incredulous glare. "Why is this happening?"

"Because the world is a crazy place, Mama," Cara said with exasperated patience.

By the time they reached the porch the dog had roused itself enough to stand at attention. "Hello, Roscoe," Cara cooed. "Who's a very good boy?"

Betsy snorted. "Good for nothing but warming the floorboards," she said, herding them all up the steps. "Come in. Come in. I have some stew on the stove and a pan of corn bread if you're ready for lunch. I know Jim's probably ready to eat his hat."

Cara's father pulled the battered Razorbacks hat from his head the moment he crossed the threshold. "I am hungry."

Wyatt stole a glance at his watch. It was early afternoon, but the Becketts had been hard at work long before the call from his commanding officer woke him. The scent of richly spiced beef stew filled the entry. He tipped his head back appreciatively and Cara's father chuckled.

"Come on in and have a bowl while you get us all caught up," he said, gesturing for Wyatt to follow his nose.

Betsy turned to Cara, her forehead crumpled with worry. "Now, I know you don't eat meat, but I forget whether cheese is okay or not."

"I, uh, yeah, it's fine, Mama," Cara said, her cheeks turning pink. "Don't worry about me. I can sort out whatever I need."

"Born to raise beef cattle, but the minute she stepped foot in California she turned vegan on us," Jim Beckett blustered.

"It didn't happen the minute I moved to California," Cara shot back. "Like every other red-blooded college kid out there, I lived on pepperoni pizza and pad Thai for the better part of four years."

She turned toward Wyatt and rolled her eyes dramatically. He couldn't help but wonder if he was there to protect her or act as referee.

"But I'm not vegan anymore. I love dairy too much."

"I should ship you off to the Bakers. They can keep you in milk and cheese if my beef isn't good enough for you," her father grumbled as he pulled out a kitchen chair. "Have a seat, Officer Dawson. Tell me what you plan to do to catch the jerk who sent that email," he ordered.

Wyatt fought back a smirk. Jim Beckett was clearly a very focused man. He wondered what Cara and her father would say if he attributed her ability to maintain balance and stay centered to him. Before he could get himself settled, Cara jumped in, acting as his self-appointed public relations representative.

"Actually, it's Special Agent Dawson, Daddy. Wyatt is a member of the Cybercrimes Division."

"Cybercrimes?" Betsy repeated as she ladled up bowls of stew. "Sounds fascinating."

"Betsy loves watching those crime shows. The ones with all the DNA testing," Jim said with a nod. "It is amazing what they can figure out with nothin' more than a few hairs or a drop of blood."

"You like them too," his wife shot back.

"Yes, uh, technology has helped in some incredible ways." He cast a glance at Cara and found her reaching into a high cabinet to pull down a jar of peanut butter. Her sweatshirt rose as she stretched, exposing a couple centimeters of skin, and Wyatt felt compelled to shift his gaze back to her father. "I deal more with the ways it hasn't helped," he admitted with a wry smile and apologetic shrug.

"Like the email," Betsy said, juice flying from her ladle as she pointed it at him.

"Exactly." Wyatt surreptitiously wiped the droplet of scalding stew from his cheek as he debated what information to divulge. He didn't want to panic the Becketts, but he also needed them to be on their guard. "And you did exactly the right thing by not replying to or forwarding the email, Mrs. Beckett."

"Pssht. Call me Betsy," Cara's mother said as she plunked a bowl down in front of him. With a quick intake of breath she drew back as if she'd burned her hand, a worried frown bisecting her brows. "I didn't ask. Do you eat meat, Special Agent Dawson?"

"It's Wyatt, and yes, ma'am. I love stew."

"Oh, good," she gushed, clearly relieved. "I poured tea for everyone, but if you want something different—"

"Tea's great. Thank you."

He picked up the spoon Betsy placed on a paper napkin, but waited until Cara and her mother joined them at the table to dig in. Cara darted a glance in her father's direction and rolled her eyes. James had already depleted half his bowl. By his daughter's bemused expression, he gathered this was the norm in the Beckett household.

"Help yourself to some corn bread," Betsy invited, gesturing to a napkin-lined basket she'd placed at the center of the table.

Cara raised an eyebrow, smirking at the basket of warm corn bread as she slathered peanut butter on a saltine. Apparently the presentation of the corn bread was not a part of the norm. He smiled as he helped himself to a wedge of the warm bread, then crumbled some into his stew.

"Thank you. It all smells delicious."

"If you ask me, everything smells fishy," James declared, not looking up from the depths of his bowl. "Why don't you tell us what the heck is goin' on here?"

"Jim, let them eat their lunch in peace," Betsy admonished.

Wyatt met Cara's eyes across the table. She swallowed the cracker she'd been chewing, then washed the crumbs down with a gulp of sweet iced tea. When she was ready, she folded her hands in front of her and angled her body to look her father directly in the eye.

"I'm not sure if you're aware, but my partners and I have decided to take our company public. We'll make a number of shares available for the public to buy on the stock market," she began.

"I know what goin' public means," James growled. "I'm

not uneducated, and no matter what you think of this place, your mother and I don't live under a rock."

"I know, Daddy," Cara said with the wary patience of a person who has covered this ground before. "Okay, so I guess you know it means I'll make a lot of money when it happens. On paper, at least."

"I told you from the beginning, this whole thing is like a house of cards," James started. "Monopoly money. It's all paper printed up in New York City and assigned a value by some…guru who pretends to know the value of air."

Cara tensed and Betsy cringed. This obviously wasn't the first time they'd heard his opinion on Cara's business.

James waved his hand in the air like he was wielding a magic wand. "How can you build anything real without hard assets? Land, buildings, equipment, cattle—"

"Cattle you take to market and sell at a price set by demand on the commodities market," Cara interjected. "A made-up number conjured by the beef oracle of the sale barn."

"Actually, companies like LYYF and other web-based businesses do have real assets. Intellectual property, patents, trademarks and copyrighted catalog are all tangible and valuable assets," Wyatt interjected smoothly. "There's also licensing, subscription and franchising." James opened his mouth to argue, but Wyatt shook his head. "But we're not here to debate the valuation of Cara's company. We're here because your daughter has become the target of some very real threats."

Cara's father's jaw snapped shut and a hush fell over the room. Wyatt nodded to Cara. "Go on. Tell them."

"I started getting messages online. Which, to be honest, is not unusual. Women are not particularly revered in technology circles. There's a small, but vocal, faction of people out there who don't believe I should be a full partner in

LYYF because I didn't contribute to the technological side of its development."

"But it's your face out there," Betsy countered. "Your voice people want to hear."

"Thank you, Mama."

Cara sighed and reached for another saltine even though the rest of them had stopped eating. She smeared creamy peanut butter onto cracker after cracker, setting them out in a row as she detailed the threats she'd been receiving, the attack on her neighbor and finally her flight to Little Rock and the events of the past twenty-four hours.

"Oh, my Lord, Cara," Betsy said, pressing one horrified hand to her chest and covering her mouth with the other.

James Beckett sat with his fist clenched tight and his head bowed. Silent. Unmoving. And seething.

"You can rest assured we have our best people working on the case," Wyatt said, speaking up for the first time since Cara started her recitation.

"Your best people?" James lifted his head, his jaw set and his eyes alight with the need to take action. "What about the FBI? Shouldn't they be working on this? She was kidnapped, for the love of everything holy," he cried, shoving his chair back and jumping to his feet.

Wyatt didn't move. If he were to get up too, it would only stoke Cara's father's ire. What they needed now was de-escalation. Calm. Sanctuary.

In other words, they all needed to take a deep breath.

"We are liaising with agents in the FBI field office, but since Ms. Beckett has been recovered unharmed and no one crossed state lines, they are deferring to the state police as lead on the investigation. Of course, we have full access to any resources they have when it comes to the identification and apprehension of the man who abducted her."

"I have every faith in Special Agent Dawson and his associates," Cara announced.

Wyatt did his best to mask the surprise and pleasure he took from her endorsement. Still, it was good to hear.

"And I promise you, we have been taking the case quite seriously." Wyatt glanced over at Betsy and flashed his most winning smile. "Even without the nudge from the lieutenant governor's office."

"Lieuten—" James started then stopped on a grunt, shooting his wife a sidelong glare. "Naturally, you called your old pal Paul for help."

"I told you I called him," Betsy said, rising from the table. She picked up her own barely touched bowl, then snatched James's nearly empty one from his place.

"You think I couldn't have called someone?" James demanded. "Dewey Roarke is a senator, for crying out loud, and we've been buddies since we were seven. We could have called him."

"Dewey is a state senator, and he's *your* buddy," Betsy countered, dropping the bowls into the sink with a clatter. "You were out at the barn when I saw the email, and I called who I knew to call."

"Good old Paul Stanton, always ready to ride in on his white Cadillac."

"I called you first," she shot back. "It took you forty-five minutes to get back to the house."

"I was in the middle of feeding—"

"Hey," Cara shouted, cutting through their bickering like a hot knife through butter. "It doesn't matter who called who. I didn't need anybody to ride in to rescue me. I'd already rescued myself."

Mr. and Mrs. Beckett both fell silent. Betsy turned toward

the sink, gripping its edges for support. James slumped, his broad shoulders sagging and his hands falling limp to his lap.

"You must think we're awful," Betsy whispered, shaking her head side to side.

An awkward beat passed, then Cara asked, "Me or Wyatt?"

A watery laugh escaped Betsy Beckett. "Both."

"Oh, Mama." Cara slid out of her chair and went to wrap her arm around her mother. Betsy's shoulders shook until Cara pressed her cheek against her mother's back. "I love you even when you're awful. It must be nice to know Daddy's still a bit worked up over the guy who took you to a dance back when you all still had a feathered hairdo."

Betsy choked out a laugh, and James moved to them as if they were magnetized. Soon, both women were engulfed in the larger man's arms again. "I hate he drives a nicer car than me," he grumbled into his daughter's hair.

"I'd buy you whatever car you want," Cara said, her voice muffled. Gradually, their family knot loosened, and Cara swiped at her cheek. "I'd even shell out for one of those enormous pickup trucks killing the planet."

"You know I have no use for a truck too pretty to haul hay," her father answered gruffly. "Let's sit down. I need to hear more about what started all this."

Before they could resume their places, Wyatt's phone rang. He checked the caller ID and saw it was Emma Parker. She was calling instead of sending a message. He could only guess something big was happening. "Excuse me for a moment, please," he said, scooting his chair back. "I need to take this."

Wyatt didn't wait to see if the Becketts were put off by his abrupt departure from their table. Nor did he look back. "Dawson," he said in a low voice, hurrying back through the living room toward the front door. The screen door didn't squeak when he pushed it open, and old Roscoe didn't stir from the patch of sun on the porch. "What's happening?" he asked as he ran down the shallow steps.

"We know who the guy is," Emma informed him without preamble.

"What? How?" Wyatt pushed a hand through his hair, all too aware he was firing questions faster than she could field them, but unable to stop. "Are you sure it's him?"

"We got latent prints off the steering wheel and gearshift, but those could have been anyone's since it was a rental car. But we had two different prints match with some we lifted from her phone."

"Is he in the system?"

"He is. Permitted for concealed carry," she informed him.

"Seems like everyone is these days," he grumbled. "This joker have a name?"

"Yes. Gerald Griffin. Thirty-eight. Residence Garland County, outside Hot Springs."

"Okay." Wyatt gave the back of his neck a squeeze, then let his hand fall as he turned back to take in the scope of the Becketts' ranch. "I guess we need to start looking for good old Gerry."

"Found him," Parker informed him, her tone grim.

Wyatt froze, his gaze locked on the overfed dog napping on the porch. "You answered fast enough to make a guy say *uh-oh*."

"I traced a debit card Mr. Griffin used to buy gas at a station near the airport."

An incredulous laugh burst out of him. "He topped off the rental before he returned it? What kind of a criminal is this guy?"

"A dead one," Emma said bluntly. "I'm thinking he filled up his own vehicle. It was parked outside his double-wide when the sheriff's deputies got there a little while ago. They identified themselves when they knocked. Mr. Griffin responded with a single gunshot."

Grimacing, Wyatt tore his gaze from Roscoe's sweet face and focused instead on the mud-splattered utility vehicle James Beckett had left parked on the other side of the fence. "He shot himself."

It was neither a question nor a statement, so Emma's only response was to expel a long breath.

"Notice anything unusual when you were poking around in his financials?"

"Depends. If you consider a series of deposits under ten K apiece made over the past few days unusual, then yes."

"I take it Griffin hadn't been getting regular direct deposits before?" he asked, knowing the question was a mere formality.

"Only his unemployment draw," Agent Parker responded tiredly.

"So we're assuming someone paid him to take her." Wyatt nodded as he allowed the pieces of information gathered to settle into place. "Safe to assume the payments came from encrypted accounts?"

"Yep. Offshore and numbered."

"And you're digging into his online activity?"

"Yeah. Nothing directly tying him to Cara Beckett, but ugh, the dude totally suffered from main character syndrome."

She scoffed in such a derisive way, Wyatt ached to refrain from asking her meaning. He already felt like he was aging out in the cyber world as it was, but he needed to know. "Main character syndrome?"

"Thinks he's the main character in every story, you know? Reading his posts you'd never guess he was driving a rusty compact and living in a run-down trailer out in the middle of nowhere."

"Delusional?"

"I'd say more aspirational," Emma hazarded. "From what I can see, grabbing Cara at the airport wasn't the only odd job he's picked up."

"Other abductions?" Wyatt pressed the heel of his hand to his forehead, wondering if this Griffin guy was some sort of kidnapper for hire.

"Nothing I can find. Lots of other things, but nothing this big. Skimming ATM cards, robbery—both commercial and residential—random credit card scams, pretty much a jack-of-all-trades."

Behind him the screen door opened, and the dog let out a low snuffling sound. He didn't need to look to know Cara was standing on the porch waiting for him. He could feel her stare.

"Okay, well, keep digging. Thanks for the intel."

He ended the call, then did a quick search for the term *main character syndrome* on his go-to slang database. A quick scan of various entries made him wonder when they'd stopped calling people plain old narcissists. He turned and found Cara sitting on the top step, feeding the dog bits of her peanut butter crackers as he gazed at her adoringly.

"News?"

The knowing trepidation in her tone told him she'd seen or heard enough to be wary. "Yeah. We identified the man who carjacked you." He crossed back to the porch, but stopped when his foot came to rest on the bottom step. "Unfortunately, when officers went to his home to speak to him, he, uh…" He hesitated for a moment, then decided there was no good way to break the news. "He killed himself before he could be questioned."

She dropped the sandwich, and her hand flew to her mouth. Her eyes squeezed shut as she murmured, "No no no no no," against her fingertips.

Wyatt scooped up the remains of the sandwich before old Roscoe could get his paws under him, then took a seat on the step beside her. "You know it is not your fault," he said, pitching his voice low.

"I know," she whispered. But it was clear from the rigid set of her shoulders she didn't truly believe what she was saying.

"I'm not even going to go into all the ways this man's choices were not your responsibility," he continued, steam-rollering whatever internal meltdown she was currently experiencing. "You need to get there yourself."

"I know," she repeated, sounding the slightest bit steadier. "Who was he?"

"A guy out of Garland County named Gerald Griffin. Sound familiar?"

She shook her head. "I'm not even sure where Garland County is."

"Hot Springs," he answered, giving her a geographic touchstone.

She shook her head some more. "No. I don't know anyone from Hot Springs. I went right from here to California for college. We only went to Little Rock to shop or catch a flight. If we vacationed, we went north to the Buffalo or sometimes Branson or Lake of the Ozarks in Missouri."

"We have to fill your parents in."

"No." The word was little more than a croak, but the stubborn set of her chin reminded him of the spat he'd witnessed at the kitchen dining table. The Becketts were fighters, it was clear. And they were tough. Resilient. Like their daughter.

"They need to know. You can't keep them in the dark.

Not only is it not fair, but also it could be dangerous. For you *and* them."

Her eyes flew open. "What do you mean?"

"Someone paid this man to take you, Cara." Gripping her upper arms, he bent until he looked her straight in the eyes. "He was paid to take you and do what with you…? We don't know."

"You think someone will come for me again," she concluded.

"We have to assume they will. And until we have the instigator in custody, I think we have to believe they are not going to be satisfied with a job half done."

Chapter Seven

Her parents' reactions to the news about the man named Gerald Griffin came as no shock to Cara, but she could tell by Wyatt's stunned expression he expected more questions than he received.

Once it was made clear the man who'd taken her was no longer a threat, her father had slapped his knees and pushed himself out of his chair, promising to be back from the south pasture before dark. Her mother murmured an insincere "Lord have mercy on his soul" before retreating to her kitchen to clear away the remnants of lunch and start preparing dinner.

For her part, she'd shown Wyatt to the guest room, told him he was welcome to set up his laptop in the seldom-used dining room and provided him with the network and password information for the Wi-Fi. Physically and emotionally drained, she retreated to her childhood bedroom, hoping some time alone would allow her to rest her mind and perhaps gain some desperately needed calm.

Gerald Griffin.

Stretched out on the twin bed she'd slept in as a girl, she tried to conjure a mental image of the man who'd turned her world upside down, and failed. How many nights had she lain in this very bed dreaming of a man sweeping her off her feet?

Too many. Then, when one actually did, he turned out to be a mercenary with a gun instead of a knight on a white horse.

Had she taken a good look at him? All she had were bits and pieces cobbled together into a jumbled composite of good and evil. Brown hair? She thought so. Polo shirt. Khaki pants. Camouflage. Safety orange.

He'd seemed so harmless. Boring. An average guy renting a boring car at a middling airport in a medium-sized city in the middle of a state most non-natives would never deign to visit.

Then he'd jumped into her car, and he was the personification of a threat, complete with a handgun and masked face. The irony of it was, he was probably less remarkable without the disguise. Maybe the addition of the disconcertingly bright safety orange made him seem more menacing.

"Breathe in," she coached herself in a whisper.

She counted to four as she inhaled, waited four more seconds, then exhaled slowly. But three rounds of box breathing later, her heart still jackhammered against her breastbone. How was it possible she managed to escape a gun-wielding maniac, but found it impossible to relax in the room where she'd spent nearly half her life?

For a moment, she missed her phone with an almost physical ache. She wished she could open up the LYYF app and disappear into dissecting and critiquing her own meditations. Or tap into someone else's reserve of Zen for a bit. She'd even go for a podcast, or a particularly juicy audiobook.

Better yet, a boring one.

A book with a narrator so monotone it lulled her to sleep.

Inspired, she rolled over to gaze at the shelves above the desk where she completed hundreds of homework assignments. She spotted the cracked spines of a teen detective series she'd devoured as a girl. On impulse, she hopped up and pulled one down. Smiling, she drank in the horrendously dated cover art as she carried it back to the bed.

Less than thirty pages in, she was sound asleep with the book spread over her chest.

A TAP ON her bedroom door startled her. She sat up, pressing her hand to her startled heart. "Come in."

The door opened a crack, but rather than her mother, Wyatt Dawson peeked in. "Sorry," he said gruffly. "I hate to disturb you, but your mother says it's almost time to eat."

Cara glanced at her watch. It was nearly six o'clock. "Wow. I sacked out."

"You needed it."

She swung her legs over the side of the bed, but before she could rise, he held up a hand to stop her. She raised surprised eyebrows as he stepped into her bedroom and closed the door. She suppressed a wholly inappropriate giggle. She'd never been allowed to have a person of the opposite sex in this room. Part of her couldn't help wondering if her mother was on the other side of the house having a complete meltdown.

"I've been on the phone with the office most of the afternoon. Listen, I'm sure you want to call your partners, but I wanted to talk to you before you speak to them."

"Okay," she prompted cautiously.

"First, I want you to return any calls from your new mobile or even mine. I don't want to take the chance of anyone tracing your parents' phone number or mine through theirs."

"Sounds reasonable."

"Second, I'd like you to, uh, obfuscate a bit about your exact location."

He looked awkward and uncomfortable, and she couldn't help wondering if it was due to his word choice or the action he was asking of her.

"Obfuscate," she repeated. "I can...but why? I assume Chris and Tom know what's happening. Zarah said she would reach out to them."

"I'm only asking you to keep things vague. How much do they know about your hometown, anyway?"

She shrugged. "They know I grew up in a rural area of a state they like to poke fun at."

He pressed. "Would they know the name of your hometown if asked?"

"No, but I've mentioned it in interviews, I'm sure. It's never been a secret. As a matter of fact, I'm sure I've referred to the peace and tranquility I've found in the Ozarks in more than a few recordings."

He bobbed his head. "You have. I guess what I'm asking is how much your partners in particular know about your folks and where they live."

She stood, suspicion blossoming into incredulity. "You suspect Chris and Tom of having a hand in this?" she asked, offended for her partners. They may not be as close as they were before success pulled them in different directions, but Cara still regarded the men as two of her closest friends.

"I have to consider it," Wyatt replied, his tone even and reasonable. "They have means and a strong motive." She must have looked as horrified as she felt because he rushed to soothe her. "I sincerely hope I am wrong because I have admired them both for some time, but as an investigator, I have to take a long, hard look in their direction. They have both the money to pay someone to terrorize you and enough followers to whip into a frenzy."

"A strong motive?" She gaped at him. "What motive? We've been friends since we were eighteen, and now all of a sudden they want to get rid of me? Have me kidnapped?"

"Someone did," he interjected. "Someone paid thousands

of dollars to a guy you've never met or heard of but happens to live in your home state to grab you at the airport. Someone who knows you well enough to know your schedule. Your movements."

"They didn't know where I was going."

"As far as you know," he shot back.

He crossed his arms over his chest, straining the shoulder seams of his shirt. Cara looked away. She knew he was speaking the truth, but for the first time in her life she was learning that the old cliché about how the truth could hurt underplayed the sensation. *Hurt* was not a harsh enough word for the searing pain a few stark facts inflicted.

"Your abduction wasn't random. It wasn't a crime of opportunity motivated by robbery, like most carjackings. Gerald Griffin was waiting for you. He took you. You said it yourself. You offered him money and the car, told him to take what he wanted. He said you were what he needed. Why? What did a man you've never met need from you?"

"I don't need you to remind me," she snapped.

"No, but you do need me to help figure out who's behind all this and make them stop," he responded.

She closed her mouth so hard her teeth clacked. Cringing, she crossed her arms over her chest and leaned her head against the door frame. "I know, but I—"

She took another big gulp of air to center herself, then did exactly what she encouraged people who used their app to do. She asked for exactly what she needed.

"Can we not tonight?" Her voice trembled, but she squared her shoulders and let her hands fall to her sides, standing her ground. "I understand time is of the essence, but for tonight, one night, can we eat my mom's pot roast and talk cows with my dad? My brain is tired. I'm on anxiety overload. I need to…be for a few hours." His broad shoulders rose as he inhaled. She rushed into the breach. "I promise we can start fresh in the morning."

Wyatt allowed his cheeks to fill before he let the oxygen seep out between parted lips. "Okay. We can wait until morning."

"Thank you," she said, clasping her hands over her heart.

He started to turn away but froze as if remembering something important. "Wait. You don't eat pot roast."

Cara inclined her head in acknowledgment. "Nor will I eat the potatoes and carrots cooked with it."

"You're going to starve here," he grumbled.

She smirked, both tickled and touched by his grudging concern. "I won't, I promise. We live in the middle of nowhere. Mom keeps the pantry well stocked and I'm sure the freezer in the cellar is filled with good stuff put up from her summer garden. I'll throw something together."

He gave another one of those slow, thoughtful nods. "I won't grill you any more tonight, but tomorrow, I need everything you can give me."

"Deal," she said with a brisk nod. "Were you able to get set up okay?"

"The connection out here must be bouncing off a satellite launched during the Ice Age."

"Slow, huh?"

"Glacial. But steady so far." He held up his crossed fingers. "I'm getting surprisingly good reception on my phone, though."

She nodded, then reached past him to open the bedroom door. "Yeah. Much faster to build cell towers than to run fiber-optic cable up here."

"If I need to speed things along, I may run into town to get a wireless router," he said as he followed her down the hall to the living area.

"I hope you realize running into town from here will likely mean going back to Conway or heading up to Harrison," she warned. "Maybe Clinton, but I doubt it."

"I figured. But I haven't reached the level of frustration where I feel the need to shop," he said with a chuckle.

Cara smiled at the attempt at levity. "Well, if the urge does overcome you, the router's on me. I keep offering to upgrade things for them, but Mom insists she only uses the computer to place supply orders and check email."

"She told me she plays a mean game of online mah-jongg," he informed her as they passed through to the kitchen.

"Does she now?"

Cara raised her eyebrows when she spotted the woman in question transferring a hunk of cooked beef onto a serving platter usually reserved for Thanksgiving. Biting back any commentary about houseware choices, she crossed to the counter and pressed a kiss to her mother's cheek. "I'm sorry I fell asleep. You should have given me a shake. I would have helped."

Her mother's mouth curved into a pleased smile and Cara stayed where she was, inhaling the familiar scents of home cooking mixed with Chanel she bought for her mother each Christmas.

"You needed rest," her mother said in her usual no-nonsense tone. "I made you a sort of stir-fry." She jerked her chin at the sauté pan brimming with a jumble of colorful garden vegetables. "Used a bit of oil, some soy sauce and some all-purpose seasoning. I also have some rice. It's the boil-in-a-bag kind, not the fancy stuff," she warned.

"Sounds great, Mama," Cara said, then gave her mother another impulsive peck on the cheek. "And I don't need rice, regular or fancy. But thank you."

Cara wasn't sure if these unexpected concessions to her

dietary choices were because Wyatt was here or if her mother was simply glad some strange man hadn't made off with her only child. Nor did it matter. She appreciated the effort.

"Your father is getting washed up," Betsy informed her. "If you'll get Wyatt whatever he'd like to drink with supper, I'll get this to the table."

"Here. Let me," Wyatt said, stepping up and extending his hands to take the platter.

To Cara's surprise, her mother acquiesced without even a token protest.

"Sweet tea okay for everyone?" she asked, turning to the fridge. It was a rhetorical question as far as she and her parents were concerned, but she didn't know Wyatt well enough to presume.

"We also have milk, water and what appears to be a lifetime supply of fruit-flavored carbonated water," she called.

"It was on special at the store. Buy two, get one free," her mother said with a sniff.

"Tea is fine for me, but—"

Wyatt trailed off as Cara pulled a pitcher filled with sweet tea from the fridge. But when she turned, she found him standing beside the round kitchen table where they'd eaten lunch looking perplexed. She quickly ascertained the cause for his concern. The table she and her parents had used for most meals had always been big enough for the three of them, but now, with the addition of a place setting for Wyatt, there was no room for the serving platter.

"I'm sorry I've taken over your dining table." He turned to her mother, a deep furrow of consternation bisecting his brows. "If you'll give me a minute, I can get things cleared—"

"Oh, for heaven's sake," Betsy interrupted, then pushed past him to remove the wooden napkin holder with its nested salt and pepper shakers to make room. "There." She gave him a brisk nod. "We never eat in there anyway." She pulled Cara's plate from her usual spot. "You can fill your plate at the stove, can't you, Sweets?"

"I can."

Cara was pouring tea over crackling cubes of ice when her father appeared, freshly showered and changed into clean clothes. With his damp hair combed and the remnants of his summer tan offsetting his blue eyes, Cara caught a glimpse of the handsome young man who'd wooed and won the heart of Elizabeth Watts. Her parents were an attractive couple. One day in an LA spa and they could easily shave twenty years off the birth dates shown on their driver's licenses.

She listened with half an ear as she filled her plate at the stove. Their conversation was so casual, so normal, it made her hands tremble. This time the day before, she'd been diving out of a moving vehicle. Now her father was naming off random items he wanted her mother to add to their supply list. Yesterday, a strange man named Gerald Griffin had been alive and well and pointing a gun at her. Today, he was dead, and her mother was pushing food on a handsome special agent from the state police.

Staring down at the kaleidoscope of vegetables on her plate, Cara focused on the vibrancy of their colors. Rounds of bright orange carrots, red pepper and yellow squash were offset by dark green zucchini and pale chunks of cauliflower. She was safe. She was home. Her mother had made this gorgeous stir-fry for her, and she was grateful. More grateful than she could say. Wetting her lips, she grasped the plate hard enough to mask her terror as she turned to join them at the table.

She wouldn't let whoever was doing this steal these precious moments from her. She would pass the few hours in peace, then tomorrow morning she and Wyatt would put their heads together and start figuring things out.

Forcing a smile, she placed her plate on the table and dropped into her chair. When she was sure she had the shaking under control, she reached for her glass and gulped the sugary sweet tea. As the cool liquid soothed her parched throat, she couldn't help thinking about how horrified her friends back in La-La Land would be if they knew she was sucking down tea brewed with leaves trapped in bags with little tags and sweetened with no less than two cups of refined white sugar.

Wyatt's phone rang and they went still.

"I'm sorry," Wyatt murmured, but they all knew the apology was both reflexive and performative. Of course he would take the call.

"It's almost as if people are aiming for our mealtimes. Go on," her mother encouraged, but her smile was nervous and forced. "We want to know everything we need to know."

But do we? Cara thought as Wyatt rose, swinging his leg over the sturdy wooden chair and pulling his phone from his pocket in a fluid motion now familiar to her. She placed her cutlery across the edge of her barely touched plate. She stared down at the brightly colored dish her mother had gone to the trouble of preparing for her, knowing she wouldn't manage another bite. Her stomach was too sour. Her throat bone-dry.

Betsy reached over and covered Cara's hand with hers. "Try to eat something. You need your strength."

Across the table, her father sat with his knife and fork clutched in each hand. "What do these people want?"

"Honestly? I don't know," Cara confessed.

"Is it money?" he persisted, jabbing his fork into his slice of roast a mite too forcefully. "They asked for ten million dollars in the email." He snorted. "Who could possibly come up with so much money?"

Cara bit her bottom lip. She didn't know how to tell her father she could. If she were to sell her portion of LYYF to Chris and Tom now, she'd be able to cover the ransom demand and still have money left over. And if she waited until after the company went public…well, according to Chris, ten million would be little more than pocket change.

As if reading her mind, her mother zeroed in on her. "Do you have that kind of money?"

Uncomfortable with the topic of money in general and feeling cornered, Cara squirmed in her seat. "I, uh," she started. Her father stopped chewing and stared at her as if he'd never laid eyes on her before. Caught in his steady blue gaze, she confessed, as always. "Not, um, you know, liquid."

Her dad gently lowered his silverware to his plate and pulled his napkin from his lap, never breaking eye contact. "But you have access to large amounts of money?"

Cara cringed inside. She'd spent most of her adult years downplaying the perceived extravagance of her California lifestyle. Particularly in the three years since the app went stratospheric. She'd sent them photos of her charming little house on Sunset Drive, but she never told them she'd paid nearly two million dollars for fifteen hundred square feet of space. It wasn't the kind of math people who clip coupons and pride themselves on canning homegrown vegetables and preserves would understand.

"I do," she replied, but added nothing more. Thankfully, Wyatt reappeared and the subject was dropped. "What's happening?"

"Not a lot. I guess Chris Sharpe has left for New York. Something about meetings with some fund managers before the stock offering. Emma says she spoke briefly with Tom Wasinski, and he says he'd like you to call him."

"Nothing more on tracing the money?" she asked as he reclaimed his seat.

Wyatt settled his napkin into his lap. "No, we've hit a dead end on the numbered accounts, but Emma is monitoring chatter on a couple forums she thinks Griffin was active on, and I have some other angles I want to track after dinner." He picked up his fork again. "I'm sorry for the interruption."

The rest of dinner passed in fits and spurts of congenial small talk. After they were through, Cara helped her mother with the dishes while her father saw to Roscoe's evening kibble and Wyatt retreated to his laptop. She was settled in the den with her parents watching a police procedural when he reappeared, looking rumpled and worried.

"Anything?" she asked, motioning for him to join them.

He skirted Roscoe's enormous orthopedic pet bed as he stepped into the room. The dog gave him a cursory snort as he passed. "Nothing we didn't already know. Countersurveillance on your accounts is running as it should," he reported, taking a seat on the opposite end of the sofa. "Nothing has popped yet."

The detective in the television show started rattling off a list of supposedly damning physical evidence they'd collected during a cursory search of the victim's sister's bedroom, and Wyatt let out a disdainful scoff.

Cara and her mother looked over at him, surprised by the interruption, but her father was the keeper of the remote. The moment the scene cut to a commercial, he muted the volume and shifted in his recliner to look directly at Wyatt.

"I take it things don't tie up so neatly in the real world," he said with a nod to the television.

"Most of the testing they mentioned doesn't exist. Or, if it does, it either produces results too unreliable to use as evidence or is so expensive most municipalities couldn't afford to implement it," Wyatt explained. "Good physical evidence is much harder to come by than fictional."

"I can't believe you dare to sit here and spoil one of our favorite shows," Cara accused.

Wyatt raised his hands in surrender. "Not another word," he promised, a smile playing at the corners of his mouth.

"I think it's far more interesting to know what's real and what isn't," her father interjected.

"Jim is hooked on those true crime documentaries they show on CineFlix." Betsy shuddered. "I prefer my crime scenes off camera and the bad guys rounded up at the end of an episode." She gave him a wan half smile. "I don't suppose it happens very often in the real world."

Cara shot him a look, hoping he'd tread carefully. Given the circumstances of their visit, the last thing she wanted to do was add to her mother's worry by piling on depressing crime statistics.

"You'd be surprised," Wyatt said, crooking his arm on the back of the sofa and angling his body in the direction of her parents' matching leather recliners. "In most cases, things are so obvious they wouldn't make for good television."

They finished out the hour and by unspoken agreement segued right into the next episode. "Tell us where they get things wrong," her father prompted as they joined the investigators on the scene of yet another grisly murder.

"I have to tell you, I've been to relatively few crime scenes," Wyatt warned. "I'm more the guy back in the office pulling the background reports or analyzing data."

"Fake it," Cara said out of the corner of her mouth. "I promise we won't know the difference."

So he did, and for the next hour, the three Becketts peppered poor Wyatt with all manner of questions, doubts and pie-in-the-sky theories as to the unraveling of the crime. By the time the case was resolved, the four of them were exhausted from poking holes in each other's theories. And Cara was able to forget she was the subject of an ongoing investigation.

For a few hours, at least.

Chapter Eight

Cara awoke to five young men dressed in an assortment of leather pants and jackets gazing down at her, each one smoldering harder than the next. She rubbed the sleep from her eyes, then rolled them as she recalled Wyatt's smirk when he saw the old poster tacked to the wall of her childhood bedroom. Fixing her gaze on her longtime favorite, she whispered, "Don't worry, guys. He's jealous of our love."

It was early. The light coming through the partially open blinds was the dusky rose of dawn. Reaching out, she switched on the milk glass lamp on her bedside table. Gold incandescent light flooded the room, and idly, Cara wondered when her parents changed the bulb. Probably not long after she'd stopped gazing longingly at her teenage crush each night before she drifted off to sleep, she figured.

Lifting her arms over her head, she indulged in an extravagant stretch. It felt so good, she laced her fingers together and pressed her open palms toward the ceiling. The next thing she knew, she'd fallen into a rhythmic four-count breathing pattern, her gaze fixed on the blooming sunrise.

She heard her parents moving around the house. The rumble of an ATV engine signaled her father's imminent departure. When it faded into the distance, she closed her eyes and listened hard for any clue as to whether her mother had gone with him to the barn. The clank of cast iron against the stovetop grate rang out with the promise of breakfast.

Cara smiled as she sank into the moment, feeling more centered than she had in weeks. It always felt good to come home, even if she hated admitting it.

The sky morphed from peachy pink to pale violet. Memories of running through the back door of a simple clapboard farmhouse that used to stand less than a quarter mile up the lane came flooding back. The slap of the screen door. The scent of fresh-baked bread. Sheets snapping in the stiff breeze whistling around the tree-covered mountains and through the valley.

She loved her grandparents' house. The old house, as it was called. There was always a pan of leftover biscuits on the stove. Whatever wasn't eaten at breakfast would be gobbled up with whatever Grandma tossed together for lunch. Or dinner, as she'd called it.

After Granddad died, Grandma moved up to the new house with Cara's parents. Her dad claimed the old house was falling down around her ears, but Cara didn't see it. When you're a kid, you don't think about drafty windows, rotting floorboards on the porch or dripping pipes.

Grandma June brought little more than her cast-iron skillet and her love of all things Hollywood with her to the new house. She slept in the room Wyatt currently occupied until the day she passed. They watched old movies together well after her parents had turned in. When she was small, Grandma June happily paid a shiny quarter for a ticket to whatever living room production Cara cooked up in her head. She'd helped Cara run lines for every school play or drama club soliloquy.

Her grandmother was the one who'd dipped into her life savings to cover Cara's airfare to California. Her gran was the first person she'd called when she'd thought she'd blown an audition or got a callback for a second look. When she passed, Cara'd spent the entire flight home sobbing into a wad of paper napkins a kindly flight attendant had provided while the businessman next to her pretended not to notice.

In her absence the old house had fallen into even more disrepair. Sitting empty, there was water damage. Rot. Termites. Black mold. When it was demolished, Cara was hurt beyond reason. She accused her parents of tearing down the best parts of her childhood. Trips home became less frequent. Phone calls were kept brief and perfunctory.

She opened her eyes, a fresh surge of anger and betrayal coursing through her veins. If they had only waited a few more years, she could have had the old house restored. But she knew such wishful thinking was fruitless. Her parents would still have been saddled with the upkeep on a house she'd visit once, maybe twice a year. She shook her head, dismissing the thought and the rush of emotion it rode in on.

Her father had done what he needed to do.

Resolved to make the most out of this unexpected time with her parents, she swung her legs over the side of the bed. The floorboards were cool underfoot. She reached for the hooded sweatshirt she'd hung on a bedpost and pulled it on over the T-shirt she'd slept in. By the time she shimmied into yoga pants and some socks, the tantalizing scent of bacon drifted down the hall.

She closed her eyes and drew from the well of inner strength, hoping it would allow her to withstand temptation. Of all the foods she'd eschewed when adopting a vegetarian diet, bacon had been the hardest habit to break. Turning the doorknob, she stepped into the hall, promising herself an enormous bowl of old-fashioned oatmeal topped with brown sugar and pecans.

The guest room door opened, and Wyatt poked his head into the corridor. She smiled when she saw one side of his hair was still artfully rumpled, while the other appeared to be suffering a near terminal case of bedhead.

"Do I smell bacon?" he asked, darting a hopeful look in her direction.

"Undoubtedly," she replied. "Dad usually only has a cup of coffee first thing. He'll come back in for breakfast once the cows are fed and turned out."

He pointed to the bathroom door. "Do I have time to shower?"

She nodded. "Yeah. I'll go help Mama and take mine after we eat."

He gave a quick nod then ducked back into the bedroom. Shoving her hands into the pockets of her sweatshirt, she shuffled through the house, her shoulders hunched against the autumn chill.

Cara found her mother fishing strips of crisp bacon from Grandma June's skillet and smiled as she listened to her hum an old Beatles song. Not for the first time, Cara thanked the heavens she'd inherited her father's ear for music. Her mother couldn't carry a tune in a paper bag.

"Mornin', Mama," she said, falling back into the easy vernacular of her youth. "Can I help?"

"Morning, Sweets," her mother said, turning from the stove with a wide, guileless smile. "I've got bacon, eggs and toast." Her smile faded and she cast a worried glance in the direction of the bedrooms. "I hope that'll be okay with Wyatt."

"I'm sure it will be," Cara assured her. She moved to the cupboard where the coffee cups were kept and pulled down the biggest one she could find. "He smelled the bacon."

Her mother wiped her hand on the crumpled dishcloth beside the stove and nodded. "I won't start the eggs until your daddy comes in, but what am I gonna feed you?"

Cara bit her bottom lip and refrained from shaking her head. Every meal, the same despairing question. "I was hoping for some oatmeal," she said as she poured the rich, black coffee into her mug. "And maybe a handful of pecans if you have some stashed somewhere?"

Her mother gave an indelicate little snort. "You can have more than a handful. Those trees your granddad planted dropped enough to feed an army of squirrels this winter."

"Then I definitely won't starve." Cara cradled the mug in both hands and took a cautious sip of the steaming brew.

Thirty minutes later, the sun was up, Wyatt had emerged fully dressed, her father had returned from the first of his morning chores and Cara was doctoring a steaming bowl of cereal. She could feel her father's gaze on her as she swirled a liberal sprinkling of brown sugar and cinnamon into the oats before dropping chopped nuts into the mixture.

"Would you like some of my oatmeal, Daddy?" she asked without looking up. Her father hated hot cereal. Always had, always would, he'd proclaimed on more than one occasion.

He picked a strip of bacon cooked shy of burnt off his plate and held it out to her. "Wanna bite, baby girl?" he taunted, his voice morning gruff.

Cara smiled. "No, thank you," she replied sweetly, looking up in time to see a puzzled expression cross Wyatt's face. "It's a thing we do," she explained.

Their customary exchange complete, her father pierced the orange-yellow yolk of his perfectly fried egg with the corner of a piece of toast, then pinned Wyatt with a stare. "So tell me, what is it you do exactly?"

She wanted to object to the blunt question, but Wyatt's

quiet chuckle assured her there was no offense taken. On the contrary, he seemed bemused.

"Do you want the big picture version or the dreary details?"

Her father took his time chewing his toast before answering. "I want to know how whatever it is you're doing applies to keeping my daughter safe. I want to know how you're going to catch whoever's doing this to her."

Wyatt paused, giving the question serious consideration. Idly, he broke off the end of a strip of bacon, popped it into his mouth and chewed, his gaze never leaving her father's face. "Do you remember me telling you the tracing technology had far exceeded what you see on the television police procedurals?"

"Yessir," her father replied, sopping up some more of the runny yolk with his toast. "Why I'm askin'. It seems like you should be getting more answers than you have."

"We do have answers. We simply don't know how they fit together yet. We know what's happening. We know how they're surveilling her. We know what's being said online and by whom in many cases. We even know where some of the communications have originated."

Her mother spoke up. "If you know who and where they are, why aren't you going after them?"

"Because most people don't use landlines anymore. We can ping whichever towers a cellular call is coming from, or trace the IP address of a message, but the technology is mobile now." He shrugged. "And even if whoever is posting these things is sitting in the parking lot of a police station, the most we can do is question them. What they say is protected under their First Amendment rights."

Wyatt said the last with an edge of rancor, but her parents responded with true outrage.

"People can't go around publicly threatening people," Betsy argued. "Isn't it some form of terrorism?"

Her father dropped his fork with a clatter. "What if there's evidence those threats are credible? Someone abducted her at gunpoint."

"We have no evidence connecting Gerald Griffin to any of the threats against Cara. From everything we've uncovered, he was hired help."

"Hired help," her mother repeated. "What a world we're living in."

Cara reached over and gave her hand a gentle squeeze. "The world is wonderful. There are some bad people in it, but there always have been." She gave them a sad smile. "The only difference is, now they have more ways to spread ugliness."

"Exactly," Wyatt said with a decisive nod. "Most online chatter is nothing more than someone using a keyboard to make themselves feel heard. They can say whatever they like about somebody, and no one can stop them. Makes the powerless feel powerful."

They fell silent for a moment, their cutlery still as they digested this unsavory bit of reality.

"I don't know about y'all, but I'm feeling pretty powerless right about now," Betsy admitted.

"Me too, Mama," Cara said softly. Then she thought about those desperate people sitting at their keyboards grasping for any opportunity to feel heard. She looked from her father to her mother, then across at Wyatt, then she smiled. "But at least we aren't alone."

CARA WAS PARKED at the dining room table pretending to write scripts for upcoming recordings, but it was hard to come across as calm and centered when her life was skidding out of control. Catching her bottom lip between her teeth, she stole another glance at Wyatt. He'd been alternating between feverish typing, glaring at his screen and muttering soft oaths under his breath for the past hour. She'd tried to engage him in conversation a couple times, but his curt answers and unwillingness to look up for more than a second telegraphed his unwillingness to engage in her procrastination efforts.

Thankfully, her phone rang.

Wyatt frowned at the name on the screen, then slid it across the table to her. "Zarah."

"Hey, Z," she said into the phone. "Hang on, let me go in the other room."

She slipped from her seat to move to the other room, but Wyatt caught her wrist as she passed, shaking his head and mouthing, "Stay."

Everything in her rebelled against his high-handed order. But the man was here because of her. He'd packed a bag, picked her up and taken up residence in her parents' house all to keep her safe. She needed to stop fighting for control. The sooner she gave herself over to the situation she was in, the sooner she'd find her way through it. Struck by her own moment of clarity, she moved back to her notebook, anxious to capture the thought. She scribbled the words "give over to get through" on the paper, then reclaimed her seat with a grin.

"What's up? Aside from you," she added, glancing at her watch. It wasn't even seven Pacific time. "You're usually still unconscious until at least nine."

"I got a call from the short-term-rental company," her assistant began, and Cara sucked in a sharp breath.

She'd completely forgotten to text Zarah to let her know she'd left the condo. "Oh! The condo." Her gaze flew to Wyatt. He widened his eyes, then grimaced. He'd clearly forgotten about checking out of the place too.

"Are you okay? What happened?" Zarah demanded. "Where are you?"

The level of panic in the younger woman's voice set alarm bells off in her head. Cara pulled the phone away from her ear, pressed a finger to her lips to indicate Wyatt should keep quiet, then put the call on speaker. "What's going on?"

"You tell me," Zarah demanded. "They called this morning saying the place was torn up and informing me they were charging the entire security deposit. Not the unit owner, but the actual company. The app," she babbled. "Little Rock police got a noise complaint. Neighbors said it sounded like there was a big fight going on. Anyway, they called the owner, but they live in Oregon. They asked the cops to check it out, and when they did, they found the door wide open and no one there. It was trashed."

She and Wyatt exchanged wide-eyed stares. Cara wet her lips, then forced a word past her suddenly dry throat. "Trashed?"

"The police sent pictures. The unit looks like someone was totally raging."

Without a word, Wyatt reached for his own phone and started typing a text.

"I left early yesterday morning and everything was fine," Cara said in a rush. "I meant to text you so you could check out, but I forgot. I'm so sorry. I didn't trash the place. You know I would never. But I packed up my stuff and left. I'm sure I locked the door after me." She darted a glance at Wyatt for confirmation. He thought for a moment, then nodded his agreement. "When did they get the noise complaint?"

"They said yesterday morning," Zarah replied. "I guess it took some time for it to get from the police back to the owner to the rental company. I freaked when I heard. I thought maybe the kidnapper was coming after you again."

"No. No one came after me," Cara said, her mind awhirl.

"Where are you?" Zarah asked again.

She opened her mouth to speak, but clamped it shut again when she caught sight of Wyatt wagging his head hard. "I, uh, I'm staying with a friend. I didn't like being alone after, um, what happened."

"What friend? Where?"

"Listen, Z, I want you to go ahead and reach out to the company and the owner and assure them I did not do this. Also let them know I'm happy to cover any damages, though. I should have let them know I was out of the unit. You have access to my cards and accounts. Do what you need to do to make this right."

"But you're okay? You're safe?" the other woman prodded.

"I'm safe."

"When are you coming home? Do you need me to book a flight for you?" Zarah persisted.

"Not yet. I'm still…decompressing. Catching up with my friend. But I'll call you as soon as I'm ready," she promised. "Would you please take care of the condo for me? I feel horrible. Maybe I didn't lock the door properly after all. Either way, at the very least, I should have let them know I was out so they could set the alarm." Wyatt made a motion for her to wrap it up. "I'll call you back later, I promise."

She ended the call before Zarah could wedge another question in and looked up at Wyatt aghast. "Someone broke in yesterday. It must have been right after we left."

His mouth pulled into a grim line. He nodded as he raised his phone to his ear. "I have a friend with the LRPD. I'm going to see what I can find out from them."

"Do you think it was this Griffin guy? I mean, could it have been?" She moved her chair a few inches closer to his, shaken and needing to feel his proximity.

"It could have," he murmured. "Need to see if the time-line fits." He held up a finger for her to hold the thought. "Yeah, this is Wyatt Dawson from the state police. Is Mark Jones in, please?" He must have been put on hold because he lowered his finger and resumed their conversation without missing a beat. "Does he return the car, gas up his truck, then go looking for you? No." He shook his head, dismissing the chain of events. "He'd go looking for you in the rental. Wouldn't want to risk anyone ID'ing his vehi— Hey, Mark," he said, his tone shifting from speculative to professional in the space of a syllable. "Wyatt Dawson. How are things?"

He listened for a minute, nodding. "I hear you. Yeah, we'll have to do that. Listen, I won't keep you, but do you think you can find out who's handling a break-in and property damage case for me? I think it's connected to an active investigation." He rattled off the address of the condo, tapping his pen against the side of his laptop. "Yeah, give them my number. Appreciate you."

Cara couldn't suppress her bemused smile.

When he looked over at her, the crease between his brows deepened. "What?"

She shook her head and wiped the smile from her face. "Nothing. I was— It's funny, is all."

"What is?"

"The weird kind of conversational shorthand guys have. If I'm interpreting your two-minute conversation correctly, you commiserated about the job, asked for what you needed, confirmed the urgency and need for response, and made some vague plan to get together—"

"Which we never will," he interrupted.

"Exactly. All wrapped up in a neat little package." She skimmed her palms together as if drying them off. "I wasn't criticizing. In fact, I was admiring your skill."

He dropped the pen to the table and leaned in to look at her. "It would have to be a wildly tight timeline for it to be Griffin," he mumbled.

She watched as he snatched up his phone and started to fire off another text.

Narrowing her eyes, she asked, "How do you know your messages are safe?" His head popped up, and for a moment he looked affronted. "I'm only asking. I mean, are they regular texts or do you have some sort of secure channel like on TV?"

"We have an encrypted network, but it's not foolproof. Some people love to crack codes," he muttered, finishing his message.

She inclined her head. "People like you and Agent Parker," she said quietly.

He studied his screen, a smile tugging at his lips as he jabbed at the trackpad. "Exactly." Then he scowled at his laptop. "I don't know how your folks can stand service this slow. Thank goodness they weren't trying to use a computer while watching CineFlix—it would crash the bandwidth. It'd get hung up right in the middle of the big forensics reveal."

His phone dinged and he glanced down at it. "Eight fifty-three a.m.," he reported. "If he trashed the place, he wouldn't have been too far behind us."

"What time did we leave?"

"Somewhere around there. I got the package with your stuff and came right to you."

"So he was doing all this in broad daylight," she murmured.

"Sometimes it's easier. People notice a commotion in the night. We're actually pretty lucky someone was home to hear it. Most people would have left for work already."

"Yeah, we're so lucky," she said with an edge of sarcasm.

He fixed her with a stern stare. "We are. We were already

gone. Now, Emma's emailing a copy of the receipt for the file." He checked his computer, then grabbed his phone. "I'm going to switch to my phone's cellular hot spot. This is driving me crazy."

A few seconds later the email with the scanned transaction from the gas station came through. He sent off two more emails before switching off his hotspot and settling back in his chair, fingers poised over the keys. "You up for running through this all again?"

Cara nodded, sitting up straighter in her chair. She spoke low and steady, keeping her breathing even as he typed a bullet-point timeline of events starting with the day she noticed an uptick in hostile messages and brought them to the attention of her partners. When they got to the attack on her neighbor Nancy and her decision to fly home to Arkansas, he slowed her down, asking her to get more granular as he added incident after incident. Her voice cracked when she recounted her decision to jump from the car, still not quite able to believe she'd done it. She hadn't realized how high and tight her voice had become until Wyatt stopped typing and reached over to cover her hand with his.

"Breathe," he encouraged. "It's okay. I've got the rest."

She nodded, dragging in a deep but shaky breath. "Okay. Okay."

"I've got you," he assured her, giving her hand a quick squeeze before releasing it to resume his typing.

Cara sagged in her seat, exhaling slow and low and feeling more confident than she had in weeks. "Yeah. We've got this," she whispered.

Chapter Nine

The rest of the day passed with agonizing slowness—on all fronts. Wyatt tried his best to refrain from grumbling about the antiquated internet service running to the house, but programs and scans he could run at high speed in Little Rock seemed to be caught in some old sci-fi movie's vision of a wormhole. Whenever he could, he switched to using his phone as a hot spot. It seemed counterintuitive to be able to get better mobile reception than satellite internet. When he mentioned as much to James Beckett on their afternoon ride around the property, the older man simply pointed to the flashing beacon on a tower poised atop the nearest hill and muttered something about Betsy's boyfriend opting for improved cell service instead.

When they returned to the house in time for Jim to fire up his propane grill, they found the fridge restocked and the two women sitting on the back deck sipping white wine.

Betsy Beckett countered her husband's raised eyebrow with a smug smirk. "I thought pork tenderloin would be nice for a change. Cara has some vegetables in there she'd like you to grill too. Oh, and I bought you boys some beer."

"Sounds good," Jim said. He leaned down and kissed his wife's cheek on his way to the door. "You pick up ice cream for dessert?"

Her lips curved into a serene smile. "You know I did."

"Perfect. I'll get things ready, then be out to get things fired up."

"I chopped and seasoned some veggies and threw them in the grill basket. Would you cook them up for me, Daddy? You're so good at grilling," Cara called after him.

Her father simply raised a hand in acknowledgment of her shameless flattery. Wyatt smiled at Cara. She looked a thousand times more relaxed than she had when he left with her father after lunch. Whether it was the wine or the nap she'd planned to take while he was out, he wasn't sure. Either way, it looked good on her. An afternoon in the fresh air had done him a world of good. Wyatt decided he was going to do his best to be sure the rest of the evening remained mellow. They all needed a bit of a breather.

"All quiet on my end," he assured her. "I'm gonna go help your dad."

She toasted him with her wine. "We expect great things from you," she called as he followed her dad into the house.

In the kitchen he found Cara's father rooting around in the back of the refrigerator. When he surfaced, he held up a package of microwavable mashed potatoes and fixed him with a challenging stare. "Life lesson—there's no need to peel, chop, boil and mash when you can have these hot and tasty in less than five minutes. Don't judge me."

"I grew up eating instant rice."

"We both believe in working smarter," Jim said with a conspiratorial nod. "Let's get this going. I'm starved."

When they sat down to dinner, her mother picked up the platter of sliced tenderloin and offered it to Wyatt as she addressed the table in general.

"Did I tell you I ran into Delia Raitt in town?" He helped himself to a piece of the meat, but before anyone could answer, she pushed the platter back at him. "Take two. Y'all look famished and you know Cara isn't going to have any."

His attention caught on how Cara stiffened at the name, he did as she asked with a murmured "Thank you," then relinquished the fork. When no one commented on Betsy's conversational gambit, he asked, "Delia Raitt? Is she someone you went to school with?"

"Mrs. Raitt was the principal's secretary when I was in school," Cara answered stiffly. "Liked to stick her nose in everyone's business."

"Well, the school district has consolidated and she's working for the superintendent now. The school system is all different now, but Delia is the same."

Jim Beckett ate steadily, oblivious to his daughter's unease. "Still nosy."

Betsy didn't seem to notice Cara's discomfiture, because she continued on without further encouragement.

"So nosy I'm surprised she doesn't trip over the end of it," Betsy said with a tinkling laugh. "Anyhoo, Dee said they've been getting calls about you."

"What kind of calls?" Wyatt asked, working to keep his tone neutral.

"Reporters, mainly. She said people have been calling and asking about your big business deal in New York," she reported, blasting Cara with a wide, proud smile. "I didn't say anything before because I wanted your daddy to hear too, but she said they're all real proud of you around there. Apparently, all sorts of fancy technological magazines have been calling and asking whether you'd come home to talk to the kids about working in big tech and what it's like to build a business from the ground up and all." She waved her fork in an all-encompassing circle before using it to stab a hunk of grilled squash.

Jim Beckett dropped his fork and stared at his wife with the open disbelief Wyatt wished he could show. "Are you kiddin' me with this?"

Betsy blinked, her smile slipping as she cast a glance at Cara, then back to her husband. "No, I'm not kidding. I told her we were proud of her too." She reached over and gave Cara's hand an encouraging pat. "And we are. Even if we don't understand it all. Aren't we, James?"

Cara's father blinked, then stared at her with such naked incredulity Wyatt cringed inwardly. "Were you drinking before you went to town?" he demanded.

"What?" Betsy asked on a sharp inhale. "No. Of course not."

"Don't you get it?" Jim shook his head. "The people callin' the school might not be reporters. They could be the people behind this whole mess." He threw his hands in the air. "Criminy, Elizabeth, we're not supposed to let anyone know she's here."

"I didn't tell anyone she's here," she retorted, shoving her chair away from the table. "I'm not a fool, and I won't be spoken to like one in my own home."

"Okay, okay," Cara interjected. "Let's all…take a breath."

Her father rolled his eyes. "Take a breath," he muttered under his. "Same mumbo jumbo for the folks willin' to pay for it."

"Fine," Cara snapped. "Let's all calm down and talk rationally," she demanded, sounding about as far from calm and rational as a modern-day guru could. "Do you think we can manage to get through one meal without bickering or picking at each other?"

Wyatt held his tongue as the older man nodded then ducked his head, reapplying himself to his plate. "I'm sorry. I didn't mean to be a jerk," Jim said quietly.

"You were a jerk, but your apology is accepted," his wife responded, punctuating her largesse with a prim sniff.

"People are calling the local school asking questions about Cara?" Wyatt asked, rephrasing the gist of the conversation.

"Yes," Betsy said, her tone markedly more subdued. She twiddled her fork, routing out a divot in the mashed potatoes he'd so painstakingly nuked. "I didn't think it sounded threatening. At least, Delia Raitt didn't make it come across like it was. She was goin' on about what a big deal Cara was now, and how proud we must be, and how she never thought little Cara Beckett would turn out to be a fancy big shot." She turned to look at her daughter. "Her words, not mine."

"Did she happen to name any of the publications they said they were calling from? Did you recognize any of them?"

Betsy shrugged, then shook her head, her smile turning rueful. "She said a couple of names, but they sounded computer-y to me." Jim snorted and her eyes lit with fire. "Like you know any better, James Beckett. You tell me the name of one of those tech blog thingies," she challenged.

"Doesn't hafta be one of those. It's been all over *Forbes*, the *Wall Street Journal*, the *New York Times*," Jim said quietly. When they all turned to look at him, he glanced up from under lowered eyebrows. "What? I don't live under a rock."

Cara ducked her head, and Wyatt couldn't help but stare as a peach-pink flush crept up her neck to her cheeks. The woman practically glowed with pleasure at this small concession from a man Wyatt himself had reclassified from remote and disinterested to quiet and observant over the course of an afternoon in his company.

"There are dozens of legitimate publications interested in profiling your daughter," Wyatt said, gently breaking the spell. "I know to those of us back here at home it may seem like she has put herself out there with LYYF, but in truth,

Cara is kind of an enigma in tech circles. Aside from her work published on the app and the social media connected to it, she has stayed out of the media. If there are interviews to be given, it's usually one of her partners in the spotlight."

"Usually Chris," her mother said with a nod. "He loves to be the one doing the talking. Always was the slick one. I remember from the time we came out there to visit."

"Chris is a talker," Cara conceded.

Wyatt jumped back in before they strayed too far off track. "From everything I can find, and believe me I have looked through all accounts connected to her, Cara doesn't put much of herself out there. Which is why she found it such a shock to have people on the internet taking such an, uh, intense interest in her personal life."

"I don't even take pictures of my food," she said with a wry smile.

"And here I thought all people put on those sites were pictures of their plates," her father said gruffly.

Cara flashed him a grateful smile and Wyatt felt his shoulders drop as the tension in the room dissipated.

"I can't," Cara said, her tone turning serious again. "I learned early on. The second I post something, a yummy dinner or a pretty blue sky, people crawl all over themselves trying to interpret the hidden meaning behind my post."

"Some people can't accept the appreciation of a pretty blue sky at face value," Wyatt said, nodding his understanding.

"Exactly. People say I'm making a statement about climate change, or take the opportunity to lecture other community members about the proper use of sunscreen. I have to be very careful about everything I post online. You never know how people will interpret it, and there's always someone waiting to pounce."

Her father shook his head in disgust. "People have nothing better to do."

"Everyone has to share their opinion," Wyatt commiserated.

"My daddy used to say opinions were like belly buttons—everyone has one, but you don't need to go around flaunting it," Betsy chimed in.

"I heard it using a different body part," her husband said under his breath.

Betsy frowned. "What body part?"

Wyatt chuckled at their byplay but refused to further the conversation. Instead, he turned to Cara. "I'm assuming the company has a publicist or PR firm they work with?"

She nodded. "All official media requests are supposed to go through a woman named Amanda Pierce. She has a boutique firm out of Palo Alto. It's called APPR," she added. "But it's not unusual for people to try to work around the process. We all get requests. Zarah fields them for me every day."

"But the bigger outlets will go through the publicist," he asserted. "I can see individual vloggers trying to get around the gatekeeper, but there'd be no reason for the *Times* or the *Journal* to do an end-around. Publications like *WIRED*, *TechCrunch*, *CNET*...they'd want everything on the record, and they'd want to be able to follow up on anything newsworthy."

"You think these people calling the school district were only pretending to be reporters?" Betsy asked, fear warring with incredulity in her voice.

Wyatt flashed an apologetic smile. "It's possible. You're sure you didn't give any hint of Cara being here?"

A deep crease of concern appeared between Betsy's brows, and she bit her lip as she closed her eyes, no doubt scouring her memory for any innocuous little comment. "I'm sure," she said at last. "She asked when we were going to California to visit again, and I said something vague about maybe over the holidays."

She flashed a wince of a smile, and Cara reached over to squeeze her hand. "You know I'd love to have you out anytime you can get away."

Both women looked at Jim, who'd remained laser focused on his food through this whole exchange. Without looking up from his plate, he mumbled, "I did like fresh-squeezed orange juice in the mornings."

Judging from the radiant smiles breaking across the women's faces, his confession was as good as a promise. "My lemon tree has started producing too," Cara informed him.

"No need to gild the lily, sweetheart," Betsy admonished softly. "We'll make arrangements for one of the Ford boys to come look after things while we're gone."

The ladies spent the rest of the meal extolling the many virtues of California living, only requiring the occasional "Huh" from him and grunts of affirmation from Jim. By the time Cara jumped up to retrieve the ice cream and bowls, the mood was considerably lighter. But the supercomputer in Wyatt's head hadn't stopped running probabilities and turning over possibilities.

After they were through eating, Jim said something about needing to make some calls. Wyatt escaped to the dining room and his laptop. A few quick queries gave him the lowdown on the newly consolidated school district and its administration. If he'd grown up anywhere else, he might have marveled at the odds of a cold caller actually connecting with a person who knew Cara and her family, but he was an Arkansan. He knew better. People born and raised in the Natural State either stuck close to home or ran far away.

He'd stuck close.

Cara had gone about as far as she could go, shy of buying a boat.

Grabbing his phone, he fired off a quick text to Emma to let her know about the calls to the school administrator's office. It wasn't critical information, but at this stage they were massing every bit of data they could and sifting through them like the tourists who spent days sieving dirt at Crater of Diamonds State Park. At this point they were hoping one of the bits of nothing they unearthed turned out to be a precious gem.

Next, he ran a general search on Cara's name. Scrolling past results for her website, links to LYYF, a Wikipedia entry and optimized entries for some of the more popular pages on the LYYF website and blog, he found an article in a respected tech journal about the company's upcoming stock option and the buzz surrounding one of the world's most popular apps. He skimmed nearly halfway through it before he realized her name had not appeared in the text. He hit the Control and F keys and typed "Beckett" into the pop-up search box.

One result returned.

Holding the arrow-down key, he scanned the screen until he found the highlighted name.

When he spotted it, he stared at his screen in disbelief. Cara, the face and voice of the LYYF app, and her 33 percent ownership, didn't garner a single mention in the body of the post. He'd found her tagged in the article's keywords, but nowhere in the lengthy, and somewhat fawning, narrative about the company's inception and astounding growth.

Skipping back to the top of the article, he checked the byline. The author was someone named Nate Astor.

He searched the site for other articles by the same author and discovered Astor was one of their main contributors.

Scrolling through his previous articles, he found two more related to LYYF.

One was a one-on-one interview with Chris Sharpe published the previous spring, and the other was an opinion piece in which he debated the value of creation versus content. About two-thirds of the way through the article, he spotted Cara's name. Biting the inside of his cheek, he read and re-read the man's hot take. Wyatt found it ironic the reporter, whose job it was to create content for an online magazine, dared to question Cara's contribution to the LYYF app's success.

"So much for solidarity, huh, Nate?" he muttered, clicking back to look through more of the man's work.

Not surprisingly, he found more than one post concerning GamerGate. He grimaced. He'd been in school when a band of misogynist jerks claimed to be on a quest to fight "political correctness" in the online gaming world by harassing, doxing and threatening female media critics and game developers with bodily harm.

"Finding anything good?"

He jumped, reflexively tipping the cover of his laptop down to shield her from his discoveries.

Cara blinked, then let out a bitter huff of a laugh. "Wow. I was kidding, but I guess you did. Was it about me, or were you looking at X-rated websites in front of my mother's Precious Moments?"

"What?" He glanced over his shoulder when she gestured to the collection of figurines on display in a corner curio cabinet. "Oh. No. You startled me is all."

"Reading something good?" She sank into the chair adjacent to his, her stare unflinching.

"Went down the GamerGate rabbit hole," he confessed.

She made an exaggeratedly horrified face. "I didn't peg you for a misogynist, so you must lean toward masochist."

"The guy who wrote the article has also done a couple on LYYF," he explained. Then, angling to face her, he asked, "Does it bother you when they leave you out of the press coverage?"

She opened her mouth, then closed it. He could almost see her swallowing whatever flip answer she kept on hand for this type of question. Rolling her shoulders back, she met his eyes directly. "Yes."

"Do you ever say anything about it to them?"

"No." She shook her head. "Not anymore."

"Why?"

She pointed to his laptop. "Ironically enough, Gamer-Gate." Folding her hands in front of her, she let her gaze slide down to the computer. "Whenever Chris or Tom even mentioned my name in connection to the business end of things, the trolls came swarming out. So we stopped." She dropped her eyes to her clasped hands, a rueful smile curving her lips. "I contented myself with the idea of being the face of LYYF, and for the most part, I like it better this way too. I get to be the star without the freaky hero worship Tom hides from, or the constant pandering Chris loves and loathes."

"But in serious publications where they're discussing the future of the business…" He trailed off, unsure he wanted to push too hard on a point that was glaringly obvious to him but may not have occurred to her.

"The lack of attribution may make people think my contributions have not been commensurate with full partnership," she concluded.

"Or give the impression your partners feel they are not," he said, fixing her with a pointed stare.

Cara unwound her tightly knotted fingers, splaying her

hands open wide and flat on the tabletop to stretch them. "At first, I was happy to have what I thought would be a shield from the vitriol," she said, nodding toward the laptop again. "But after things took off there were times I felt credit wasn't being given where credit was due."

"Did you speak to them about it?" he prompted again.

"I did. On more than a few occasions," she said flatly. "To be fair, most of the requests for interviews have been fielded by Chris. He enjoys the spotlight more than Tom."

"Enjoys it to the point of hogging it. In most of the articles I read, Tom is relegated to nothing more than a couple lines. Even then, he's spoken of as some kind of tech wizard hiding behind the green velvet curtain. You're barely mentioned at all."

"None of us got into this to be famous," she pointed out.

"But I have to assume the guys, at least, got into it to get rich," he retorted. "It was basically a run-of-the-mill personal finance app until your posts started taking off." He tapped on his phone to wake it, then opened the application. Within seconds, the Cara Beckett who'd calmed his anxieties and gently lulled him to sleep appeared. He turned the phone to face her. "You made this app what it is. Everything they built…it's all scaffolding for your genius, not theirs." He leaned in, his stare searching. "Are you trying to tell me it doesn't bother them?" When she didn't answer, he gentled his tone. "Why haven't they called, Cara?"

She shook her head. "You don't get it. Things are complicated—"

"No, I don't get it." He interrupted whatever excuse she was planning to employ to excuse the shortcomings of the men she still called friends. "And I don't see it as complicated. If my friend was being attacked from all sides, I'd be there. If my friend had been abducted at gunpoint, I'd do more than text her assistant for updates. But then, my friends aren't about to increase their wealth exponentially by taking a share of the money I may or may not believe to be rightfully mine."

"Now, wait a minute—" she began, but he held up a hand to halt her protest.

"I won't say anything more. They are your friends and your partners. You know them a thousand times better than I do," he conceded.

"I do."

"But I want you to know, as far as I am concerned, no one is above suspicion. Because you and I both know there's no enemy with better ammunition than a person's best friends."

"I understand."

"And you mentioned something about Zarah having access to your accounts. Do you mind if I do a deeper dive into your financials?" He didn't need to ask, really. He could probably hack his way into every account she'd ever opened without any trouble, but she was starting to trust him, and he didn't want to risk compromising her trust.

"My financials?"

"I only want to be certain there are no...anomalies. If people have accessed everything else, it wouldn't be much of a stretch."

"Oh, wow. I never thought." She cocked her head. "I hardly ever even look at bills or account balances anymore. Zarah has everything covered."

"Just a cursory glance," he assured her.

She nodded and looked to be about to say more when Betsy appeared in the dining room doorway.

"Come on, you two. Enough work for one day. Jim has time for one episode before he hits the hay and I want to see if you can solve the case before Detective Pemberton figures it out." She made a shooing motion, then declared, "I'm making popcorn."

With a sigh, Wyatt powered down his laptop and closed the lid. Cara showed no inclination to move. Placing his hands on the edge of the table, he pushed his chair back. "Come on. Your mom is right. We've done enough for one day."

Wordlessly, Cara followed him into the family room, where her father had an episode of a murder mystery cued up and ready to go.

Wyatt smirked when he saw the show they'd selected. "You remember I'm not a homicide detective, right?"

"Neither am I," Jim answered gruffly.

"But I bet you have a friend who's one," Cara said, petulance lacing her tone.

"I do, as a matter of fact." He turned to look at her, but she stared straight at the screen. He'd hit a tender spot in questioning the quality of her friendships with her partners, but he couldn't say he regretted doing so. If she spent even a few minutes thinking deep thoughts about her relationship with the men she's helped make rich, maybe she'd reach the same conclusion he had.

Internet bullies were thick on the ground, for certain. But no one had better motive for wanting her out of the picture than Chris Sharpe and Tom Wasinski. Everything she'd told him about her life and the lives of the two men would suggest their friendship had become distant. A relationship bearing a label bestowed by nostalgia, but in truth boiled down to a business arrangement forged by people who were little more than kids.

But it wasn't a real friendship.

"Hurry up. I have to be up in seven and a half hours," Jim called to his wife.

"Hold your heifers," she retorted as she bustled back into the room. She distributed bowls of microwaved popcorn to each of them.

"Isn't it supposed to be 'Hold your horses'?" Wyatt asked Cara, hoping to break the ice, but she remained silent.

"Not on a cattle ranch," her parents replied in unison.

Jim pointed the remote at the screen as Betsy claimed her seat beside him. The opening theme music played and he darted another glance at Cara. She sat stone-faced, her jaw tight as she glared at the television screen. In the dim light, he thought he caught the faint shimmer of tears in her eyes and looked away.

They were less than five minutes into the show before he and Jim pointed to a slick-looking charmer on the screen and declared, "That one," in unison.

"Oh, honestly," Betsy muttered as she rolled her eyes. "My grandma could have seen him coming." With a huff, she grabbed the remote away from her husband and clicked through the menu. "Go to bed, spoilsport."

Chuckling, Jim kicked the footrest of his recliner back into place and rose with a groan. "Maybe I should become a homicide detective. What time do y'all have to be at work most days?"

"Long after you are," Wyatt replied with a sympathetic smile.

"Night, all," Jim called as he dumped the remainder of his popcorn into Betsy's bowl. "Wire to stretch in the morning."

"I'll be along in a bit," his wife promised as she scrolled through the options. She paused on one featuring characters in elaborate costumes. "Oooh. Wyatt, do you like *Pride and Prejudice*? Cara and I love this one, don't we, hon?"

Wyatt smiled and nodded, stuffing his cheeks with popcorn to avoid having to say more. If watching people who carried parasols and walking sticks was what it took to get back on Cara Beckett's good side, he could take it. At least, he hoped he could.

Chapter Ten

Cara jerked out of a dream where she was hurling herself from a car being attacked by birds. Why she thought she'd be safer outside when they were pecking viciously at the glass, her conscious mind could not fathom, but there—

The tapping came again. Pushing up to her elbows, she glanced at the window first. No. Someone was pecking at her door. She blinked into the darkness, then figuring it was one of her parents coming to tell her they were off on their predawn errands, she croaked, "Come in."

The bedroom door swung inward, but Wyatt stayed firmly on the other side of the threshold, his phone pressed to his ear. She sat up in her single bed, the covers drawn up to her chin, waving him in. The last thing she wanted to do was wake her parents.

"Emma Parker," he mouthed to her, indicating the other agent was on the opposite end of the call as he stepped into her room. He glanced at the door and raised a brow. She nodded and he closed it behind him, sealing them both into the small bedroom. She hit the switch, and the glare of the ceiling light set them both blinking.

"You said someone called Cara's phone? Which one?"

Cara threw back the covers and sprang from the bed. The

display on her ancient clock radio showed it to be approaching 2:00 a.m.

"And what did they say, exactly?" he persisted. Cara scowled and tugged on his arm, but he held firm, his lips thinning as he listened. "I see. Any confirmation of damage?"

She tugged again, and he pulled away, then motioned for her to remain patient.

"What is happening?" Cara hissed between clenched teeth. She grabbed hold of his free wrist and squeezed. "Damage to what? Where? The condo?"

"Ah, okay. I see." He nodded, then gently removed her hand. "I'll let her know and call you back when we've had a chance to figure out next steps."

He ended the call, then lowered the phone, his brow furrowed with worry. "What? What is it?"

"A little after midnight Emma had a call come through to your original mobile number from the new one and thought it was odd, so she picked up."

Cara frowned. "After midnight? Is she working twenty-four-hour shifts?"

He shrugged. "We're a small department and most of our work can be done off-site. We often take our work home."

"You said something about damages. What happened?"

"The caller claimed there was a fire at your residence, then hung up. Emma checked the voice mailboxes for both numbers and found one where the caller said something along the lines of 'accidents happen when you play with fire.'"

"Play with fire?"

"Emma put in calls to the LAPD and fire departments, and was able to confirm an emergency services call to your address, but they wouldn't give any additional information and the detective assigned to your case has not returned her calls as of yet."

She let out a breathy snort. "Yeah, I can believe it. I know they have their plates full, but...yeah." She pushed a hand through her hair, and the corn-silk strands fell right back over her eye. "So what do we do?"

"Do you have anyone you can call who lives nearby, Zarah?"

Shivering, she tugged at the hem of her top, wishing she had long sleeves and pajama bottoms rather than the cotton T-shirt and sleep shorts Zarah had procured. Shifting to place one cold foot atop the other, she shook her head. "Zarah lives out in the Valley. We do most of our work virtually."

"A neighbor? Your cat people?"

Color flooded her cheeks. "We, uh... I don't have their phone numbers. Any of them," she added, looking down at her hands clasped in her lap in bewilderment. "It's not Arkansas. I've only lived there a few years and..."

He tried to pretend he understood, but the idea of not knowing at least some of his neighbors must have been almost incomprehensible to him. Little Rock was a good-sized city, but in many ways it was still as interconnected as a small town. The truth was, there were few degrees of separation between most Arkansans, and even the city folk tended to look out for their neighbors.

He cleared his throat, and plowed ahead. "Em has been on the forums." He gave her a sympathetic wince. "The scuttlebutt online is it wasn't an accident and the damage is pretty bad."

"You think someone set fire to my house?" She blinked up at him, not quite certain they were speaking the same language.

He reached past her, plucked a hoodie from the bedpost where she'd hung it and handed it to her. "I'm telling you there was possibly a fire at your residence in Los Angeles, and we have heard rumors it may have been the result of arson, and the damage is extensive. Nothing is confirmed, and no one has tried to reach out to you. Not the local officials, not Zarah or any neighbors. For all we know, this is a hoax."

Cara shrugged into the sweatshirt. "Someone is saying they set fire to my house," she repeated flatly.

He nodded slowly. "Yes."

"They said they'd burn it all down," she murmured as she huddled into the fleece-lined warmth.

"Who did?" he prompted, his brow furrowed. "Who said 'burn it all down'?"

Cara shook her head, her bewilderment turning to helpless fury. "They did." She practically spit the words. "The people sending me nasty messages and scaring my poor mother half to death. Whoever paid Gerald Griffin to pull a gun on me in an airport parking garage." She threw her arms out wide, as if gesturing to the wide array of invisible threats closing in on her. "They are doing this. Whoever *they* are."

"Until we can get confirmation from a trusted source, we need to assume these are simply rumors." He held her phone out to her. "Emma sent the number for the person she spoke to with LAFD. You need to be the one to call." She reached for the cell phone with a sticky note affixed to the glass, but he held firm for a beat too long. "It's possible they won't give you any information over the phone."

"They'll give me the information. If being a semipublic figure is good for anything, it's being recognized." She yanked the phone from his grasp.

She stared down at the name scrawled below a number with the familiar area code. Investigator Shanna Gleason. The moment the call connected, she introduced herself and, reading from the sticky note he'd handed her, asked to speak to Investigator Gleason.

A moment later a woman picked up. "ACTS, Gleason here."

"Um, hello. Yes," Cara stammered, her gaze darting to Wyatt. "Am I calling the Los Angeles Fire Department?"

"Yes, ma'am."

A huff of self-conscious laughter escaped her. "Sorry. I guess I expected you to say LAFD when you answered, but you said something else and I wasn't sure," she rambled.

"Who's calling?" the other woman asked.

"Oh, right. This is Cara Beckett. I'm calling about reports of a fire at my house on Sunset Drive in Los Feliz," she said, focusing on the facts. "I believe you were contacted by Special Agent Emma Parker with the Arkansas State Police trying to confirm there was a fire?" Again, her gaze found Wyatt's, and he nodded encouragingly.

"Yes, ma'am, I spoke with Agent Parker," the investigator on the other end confirmed.

When she said nothing more, Cara gestured her frustration at Wyatt. "Ask to put her on speaker," he whispered.

"Ms., uh, Investigator Gleason, I'm here with Special Agent Wyatt Dawson of the Arkansas State Police. Do you mind if we put you on speaker?"

There was a moment of hesitation on the other end, then a curt response. "Sure."

Cara pressed the speaker button, then nodded at Wyatt. "Investigator Gleason, this is Agent Dawson. I work with Agent Parker and am currently with Ms. Beckett. What can you tell us about these reports of a fire at her property?"

"Are you currently in police custody, Ms. Beckett?" Investigator Gleason asked. "Isn't it the middle of the night in, uh, Arkansas?"

"It is, but I am not," Cara answered, stiffening at the implication. "Agents Dawson and Parker are working on a case in which I was the victim."

"I see," the other woman answered in a cautious tone.

"Ms. Beckett has been the target of several credible threats to her safety," Wyatt informed her. "One of those threats turned into a reality when she landed in Little Rock. I am here with her now as both an investigative and protective partner." He caught her eye and held her gaze. "Tell me, what does ACTS stand for?"

"Arson Counter-Terrorism Section," she replied crisply.

"I see," he replied.

Cara only whispered, "Arson."

"You believe someone set the fire intentionally," Wyatt prodded.

"I'm afraid so. I'm happy to hear you were not in the structure at the time, Ms. Beckett. Can you confirm whether anyone else should have been on the premises in your absence? House or pet sitter? Guests?"

"No. No one."

Cara pressed her fingertips to her chin to keep it from trembling. She loved her house. It was the one extravagant purchase she'd made since the app took off, and she'd spent countless hours making it her sanctuary. Now, because some jerk hacker decided to post her address for all the trolls to see, someone had violated her sanctuary. Again.

"How bad is the damage?"

"Looks worse than it is," the woman on the other end assured her. "You'll need to contact your insurance company and get someone out there to start restoration. It may take a while, but in my estimation, the house should be habitable again."

"I'm assuming you found evidence the fire was set intentionally?" Wyatt asked.

"We didn't have to look very hard. They left gas cans in the yard. And before you ask, no, we weren't able to get any physical evidence from them. I'm assuming our firebug wore gloves."

"I see." At a loss for how to proceed from here, Cara sought Wyatt's steady reassurance again.

He nodded to her cell phone. "We'll ask Ms. Beckett's assistant to help with the insurance and getting the place secured. Has Agent Parker shared any information with you on the case we're working here?"

"Only to route all attempts to contact Ms. Beckett through your office for the time being."

"Thank you. I do have some information I can share. I think it may be helpful to you. If you would send me your email address, I will send you a link to the files. I warn you, it'll be encrypted and will ask for about everything but your blood type and the guarantee of your firstborn son."

He said the last in a lighter tone, but Cara couldn't even muster the weakest smile.

The other woman chuckled. "My son is acting every minute of his fifteen years these days, so if you want him, you are welcome to him." She paused to take a breath. "I'm curious to see what you have in your file, Agent Dawson. As long as it doesn't have one of those 'click on pictures of bridges' things," she added. "And Ms. Beckett?"

"Yes?" Cara responded in a reedy voice.

"I'm very good at catching firebugs," Shanna Gleason assured her.

Cara straightened her spine and inhaled through her nose as if taking in the other woman's confidence. "I'm sure you are. Thank you," she added, a small smile tugging at the corners of her mouth.

She ended the call but didn't relinquish the phone.

Wyatt looked down at her and sighed, his expression troubled. "Maybe I shouldn't have told you until I knew more."

"No." She sat down on the edge of the bed. "Don't shut me out. What I don't know *can* hurt me, Wyatt. It can hurt me badly. I don't want you withholding information from me."

He inclined his head. "I agree. So now you know." He stepped back, groping for the doorknob. "It's unlikely we're going to get more information at this hour."

"I guess not," she conceded.

Then she heard a muffled cough from down the hall. Her parents. Biting her lip, she looked up at Wyatt, her expression pleading. "Listen, can we keep this quiet for now? I don't want to worry my parents any more than I already have."

He nodded solemnly. "What happens in California stays in California." Wyatt held out his hand. "I'd like to hang on to the phone. Emma and I are still checking incoming messages and voicemails regularly."

She placed the device in his hand without protest. She was discovering how pleasant it could be to have a buffer between her and bad news. "Take it."

He ran a hand through his hair. "Try to get some rest. There's nothing we can do from here. We can come at this fresh in the morning."

She sank back onto her heels and smirked. "Are you going to sleep?"

"I'm going to try." He gave her a lopsided smile. "I know things start earlier around here than they do in Little Rock."

She glanced at the ancient clock radio on the bedside table. "My dad will be up and out in a few hours."

"Try to sleep. There's nothing we can do right now. Your house can be fixed, and we know you're safe here." He started to back out of the room. "We'll go after them again tomorrow."

"Right," she said, though she couldn't imagine how he planned to go after anyone. She felt like Don Quixote, fighting off imaginary foes. "We'll go after them again tomorrow."

"Good night, Cara." He pointed to the poster on her wall, then hit the light switch as he backed into the hall. "Try to get some sleep. Dream about boy bands," he added in a loud whisper.

Cara snorted and wondered why her mother had left the poster tacked to the wall for all these years. "Good night."

The door clicked shut behind him, and Cara climbed back into bed. Pulling the sheet and quilt up over her legs, she leaned back against the pillows, the hood of her sweatshirt pushing up against her ears. She yanked it up over her head and sank into it.

Trolling, threats, doxing, attempted assault, thwarted kidnapping and now arson. Uncrossing her arms, she stretched them wide before drawing them into her sides. The ceiling stared back at her. Closing her eyes, she reached deep into her bag of tricks.

It took three rounds of deep sleep meditation before she landed on a course of action. Decision made, her mind quieted and she finally drifted off.

Wyatt was up a while longer. Grumbling about the slow internet connection, he attempted to comb through the hundreds of direct messages, forum entries, social media posts and emails sent to Cara within the past month. Sure enough, he found some reference using the phrase "burn it all down" in every mode of communication. Bone tired, he created a folder titled "Fire" and added screenshots of each one to it.

When he was finished, he powered down his laptop and set it aside in favor of pen and paper. But rather than making case notes, he reached into the bag of tricks he'd picked up from the LYYF app in an attempt to clear his mind. Pen in hand, he numbered a blank page in the battered composition notebook he carried with him with numerals one through ten. Then he did his best to distill everything nagging him into a list of no more than ten bullet points to be addressed the following day.

Thoughts, hunches and random observations. He listed them all in no particular order. Everything from his suspicions about Cara's business partners to the need to talk to Jim about getting better locks installed on his doors. He noted the guest room was decorated in a trendy farmhouse scheme, but Betsy Beckett had left a poster of a boy band taped to the wall of Cara's old bedroom. He started an entry about her blue eyes, but caught himself in time to change it to a more businesslike inquiry regarding whether she wore prescription eyeglasses. Then, annoyed with himself, he recopied the list of IP addresses he'd isolated and wanted to run the next day as punishment for getting too personal.

In the end it was a mishmash of to-do items, reminders and worries a desk jockey like himself was in over his head on a protection detail. He was forgetting something. What was it?

Tapping the end of his pen against the paper, he gnawed his lip until he tasted blood. When was the last time he'd been to the shooting range? He'd been raised in duck-hunting country and firing weapons since he was big enough to hold a pellet gun, but being responsible for the safety of a living, breathing woman was a far cry from shutting down phishing schemes and heading off malware attacks.

He set the notebook aside and rolled out of bed and padded down the hall to check the door locks. If nothing else, he could cross number three off his list straight off the bat.

Satisfied they were as secure as the flimsy lock sets would allow, he returned to the guest room. The notebook teetered on the nightstand. The inside of the waistband holster he preferred took up much of the free space. He'd found an outlet for his phone charger behind the headboard. It sat charging and silent since the call from Agent Parker. He could only assume everyone was in bed. As he should be.

But his mind would not slow.

On impulse, he grabbed his phone and scrolled through his contacts until he found the number for a guy who'd graduated from the academy not long before him. For most of his career with the Arkansas State Police, Ryan Hastings had provided personal security for politicians, visiting dignitaries, sports figures and, most recently, a very high-profile heiress before retiring to start his own agency.

Having done all he could do for now, he toed off his shoes as he tapped out a quick message for Ryan to contact him at his earliest convenience, then stretched out on the bed without bothering to undress or pull back the duvet.

Wyatt stared at the ceiling for a full fifteen minutes before his flighty thoughts landed on the thing he'd forgotten. Grabbing his pen and paper, he scrawled, "Follow the money," on his list of things to do, before tossing the pad and pen on the unused pillow.

He was asleep in seconds.

Chapter Eleven

He awakened to a light knock on the door. Wyatt cracked an eyelid and was surprised to find bright autumn sunlight streaming through the window. Judging by the angle, he guessed it was early by city standards, and likely midday in ranch time.

"Come in," he croaked.

The door opened and Cara poked her head in. "Hey. I tried to let you sleep, but I couldn't wait any longer."

He sat up and swung his legs over the side of the bed. Feet planted firmly on the floor, he scrubbed the sleep from his face with his palm. "No. I should be up." He checked the time on his phone. Seven thirty. He'd slept for a few hours, but it still didn't feel adequate. "You get any sleep?"

She smirked and shrugged. "Some here, some there. Restless."

"Fretting," he corrected.

"I think I'm entitled."

Her retort was sharp enough to jolt him fully awake. "Of course you are."

"Sorry." She glanced over her shoulder, then returned her temple to its resting spot on the door frame. "My mother always says I get snappy when I haven't had a good night's rest." She paused long enough to roll her eyes. "I hate it when she's right about me."

"Parents. They think they know everything." He pushed to his feet and stretched. "I suppose yours have been hard at work for hours?"

She nodded. "Dad said if you want, he'd take you out again later."

Wyatt nodded and scratched his stubbly cheek. "I'd like that."

"They left biscuits and sausage gravy for you."

"Great." Then he caught her wording and paused. "Left? Did your mom leave?"

Cara's eyebrows shot up. "Was she under house arrest?"

"No, I thought…" He trailed off, his ears burning.

"You thought she stayed here all day making stew and doing the mending?" she teased.

"No. I mean, I know she handles the paperwork and such, I didn't know she did, uh, work out there." He hooked a thumb over his shoulder. He clamped his mouth shut. He was digging himself deeper with every single word. "I need coffee."

Cara took mercy on him. "I'll pour you a mug. Mama went to pick up some wire fencing they need for repairs. She'll be back by noon, but I warn you it's Daddy's day to cook, so it'll be cold cuts for lunch and something grilled for supper."

Wyatt inclined his head to indicate her message was received. The Beckett Ranch was an equal opportunity operation. "I'm going to take a quick shower. Clear the cobwebs."

"Go for it," she said, pushing away from the doorjamb. "I only wanted to get my phone."

"Your phone?"

"My cellular device?" she prompted. "I don't want to take the chance of anyone tracing the landline, remember?"

"Right, but who are you going to call?"

This time, only one brow rose. "Do I have to clear it with you?"

The icy edge in the question had him straightening his shoulders. "No, but it would help things if you kept me in the loop."

"I'd like to call my assistant, if you don't mind," she returned with a sniff.

As if on cue, the phone sang out its generic ringtone. Cara raised an eyebrow at him, then let her gaze trail over to the phone lit up atop the dresser. The display showed Zarah's number. "Speak of the devil. It's Zarah," she informed him, swiping to accept the call.

"Put it on speaker?" He did his best to phrase it as a request rather than a demand, but it could have gone either way. Thankfully, Cara complied.

"Hey, Z. You're on speaker and my pal Wyatt is here," she said, darting a glance at him. They'd agreed to play their relationship to one another off as friendship in case someone was listening in.

"Cara! I can't believe it," Zarah said in a rush. "Is it true it's a total loss? Your beautiful house. It was so adorable. I'm heartbroken."

Cara's eyes darted to his and Wyatt scowled. He tapped the mute button then said, "We need to think for a minute about how much you should say to people. Can you tell her you'll call her back? Let me get a cup of coffee and kickstart my brain."

She nodded, the tip of her tongue pressed against her top lip as she blinked rapidly, clearly trying to get her emotions under control before she spoke. He squeezed her shoulder, then stepped away, giving her space. "Hey, yeah, we're actually on another call. Can I call you back? I'll fill you in as soon as I can."

"Of course. Call me if there's anything you need me to do. I don't mind driving down there," Zarah offered.

"I appreciate the offer. I'll let you know when I've wrapped my head around it all."

Wyatt waved his arm to get her attention and when she looked over at him, he mouthed, "How did she know?"

"Yeah, um, Z? Did someone call you or something? I mean, how did you find out?"

She darted a glance at Wyatt and he gave an exaggerated nod. She'd hit exactly the right note of vague but focused calm. It wasn't until he saw her take a slow, deep inhale that he realized it was because she was using the same voice she used for meditations on the app.

"Find out? The news. It's all over the news," she cried. Then she caught herself. "Oh, wait. It's probably not making the local news there, is it?"

Cara pulled a face, then shook her head as she wrapped up the conversation with promises to call back.

Wyatt pulled up the browser on his phone and typed "Cara Beckett house fire" into the search engine. Within seconds he had all the information he needed. Without a word, she took the phone from his hand, her lips parting in shock as she took in the photos of what used to be her picture-perfect home.

Wyatt stared too. Though he had been the one to deem the posts a credible threat, he hadn't truly believed someone had done the deed. But they had. Whoever they were. They set fire to her house. The house he'd looked up on a popular real estate site the night before. To a guy from the mid-South, the California cottage looked high-end. Sleek, clean lines. Solid surfaces. It looked like it was built to withstand anything Mother Nature could throw at it.

Too bad there was no way to guard against the darker side of human nature.

Beside him Cara emitted a guttural groan.

"I'm sorry," he murmured, knowing the words to be wholly inadequate.

"I have to…" She fumbled with her phone. "I'm calling Zarah back."

He reached for her hand, but he wasn't sure if he was trying to stop her or steady her. "Hang on a second."

"I can't. I can't hang on," she insisted, her voice rising with agitation. "I have to get back." Zarah must have answered because Cara snapped into planning mode. "I have to get back. Can you book me a flight?"

Wyatt had no idea what Zarah's response was, but he started shaking his head. "No. You can't."

"I'm a couple hours from Little Rock, so I'd need a flight tonight," she continued, undeterred.

"Not a good idea," Wyatt insisted. He reached for her elbow, but she spun out of his grasp.

"Maybe look at flights out of Springfield, Missouri. Or the regional airport in northwest Arkansas?" she persisted. "Or even Memphis."

"Cara, it's not safe for you to go home right now," he said, raising his voice in a vain attempt to break through her stubborn streak.

She spun on him, her eyes bright with fear and fire. "It's not safe here, either."

He stepped closer to her, hoping to force her to back off from a bad plan. "You know it's better here than there. No one knows where to find you here. And even if they did, they'd have to go through me to get to you."

Their gazes clashed and locked. She lowered the phone from her ear, and for a split second he thought maybe he'd gotten through to her. But rather than pressing the button to end the call, she switched the audio to speaker.

"I can get you out of Little Rock after seven tonight. You'd connect through Dallas and get into LAX a bit after midnight," Zarah reported.

Cara continued to drill holes into him with her laser-like focus. For a hot second, he fooled himself into thinking she was coming around to seeing things his way.

Lifting the phone close to her lips, she looked him dead in the eye and said, "Book it."

She ended the call, then stepped calmly around him and stalked back to her room.

"Cara," he called, whirling on his heel. "I know those photos are awful, but you have to think this through."

But he was speaking to an empty hallway. He skidded to a halt in his sock feet, gripping the frame of her bedroom door to slow his momentum. She was riffling through one of the plastic bags of clothes.

"You can't go to California."

"I'm not going to California," she replied in a tone so placid he wondered if he'd imagined the whole phone call.

"But you—"

"I asked Zarah to buy an airline ticket," she interrupted. She pulled a pink hooded sweatshirt from the bag and snapped the tag off with a vicious yank. "I didn't say I'd be on the plane."

He blinked twice. "You're not going?"

"I'm not a fool," she said, shrugging into the hoodie.

Narrowing his eyes, he assessed the woman in front of him. "I would never mistake you for one, but do you care to clue me in on your plan?"

She started pacing the room, phone clutched in her hand and movements jerky with pent-up frustration. "I don't have a plan. All I know is some joker posted my private information for all to see, and my neighbor got attacked in front of my house. I try to get out of town for a few days, and a random guy I've never laid eyes on tries to kidnap me. I get away from him, but then, said random guy ends up dead. Meanwhile, back on the coast, someone set fire to my house, Wyatt. I don't know if they thought I was in it, or if they even cared—"

"They know you weren't in it," he interjected.

She whirled. "How do you know?"

"We're monitoring the chatter online." He pressed the heels of his hands to his eye sockets in a vain attempt to quell the throb building in his brain. "Can I please take a shower and have some coffee before we play twenty questions? We need to talk, and I can't think," he said, exasperated.

"Fine." She waved a hand at his rumpled clothes. "Go take your shower. I'll go brew a fresh pot."

"Thank you." He exhaled the words in a gust, then turned and trudged down the hall to gather his stuff. If they were going to go multiple rounds on how best to handle this fire situation, he needed to be as clearheaded as possible.

CARA POURED STEAMING coffee into two mugs as she waited for Wyatt to shower and change. The scent of her mother's fluffy biscuits still filled the kitchen. She lifted one corner of the tea towel covering the ancient iron skillet. Her stomach rumbled like distant artillery as a battle of will raged inside her. Cara knew the heavy pan had been greased liberally with the bacon drippings collected in the can on the counter. But the biscuits themselves were made from the same self-rising flour her grandmother had used, and fresh butter and buttermilk from a neighboring farm.

Nostalgia made her chest ache. The sight of those golden brown biscuits made her mouth water. Her stomach gurgled again, and she abandoned her principles.

"Desperate times," she murmured as she pulled one from the still-warm pan.

She split the biscuit, slathered it with butter and drizzled fresh honey on top before taking an enormous bite. Closing her eyes, she hummed her appreciation as she chewed. It was a taste of her childhood. A bite of a time when things were simpler. Safer.

Absently, she licked at a drip of buttery honey oozing down the side of her hand.

Cara popped the last bit into her mouth, chewing slowly as she doctored the other half. This time, she nibbled at the edge of the biscuit, letting the butter and honey flow onto her tongue as she peered out the window over the sink. The land where the old house once stood had long since been reclaimed by Mother Nature, but it was still vivid in her mind's eye.

"What's your plan?"

She jumped at the sound of Wyatt's voice, and the remains of the biscuit crumbled in her hand. Butter and honey oozed between her fingers. She'd been so deep in her thoughts, she hadn't heard him approach. Her face flamed with embarrassment and a touch of shame as she shook the clumpy mess off into the sink.

"Sorry," he said as he approached. "I thought you'd have heard me talking to Roscoe."

"No, I was..." She turned on the tap and cool water rushed out, coagulating the goo coating her hand. She closed her eyes and drew a steadying breath as she waited for the water to warm. "I was in another world."

One filled with biscuits baked in grease-coated cast iron and dusty memories. A world where she envisioned herself being the next Meryl Streep rather than an internet-famous—or infamous—voice-over artist being terrorized by internet trolls.

He lifted the corner of the towel and eyed the leftover biscuits still nestled in the pan. "These look great. My MaMaw used to make biscuits in a cast-iron skillet too. Refused to eat the kind out of a can."

His use of the pet name for his grandmother triggered an involuntary smile. "Mine too. This was her pan."

Wyatt eyed the pan covetously. "I buy the frozen ones once in a while. They're better, but not like this."

"They're okay, but so full of preservatives."

"Californian," he muttered.

Cara chuckled as she wiped her hand on the dishcloth hanging beside the sink. "Plates are in the cupboard in front of you. Gravy is in the microwave."

She scooped the remains of her sodden biscuit from the sink with a paper napkin and deposited the wad in the trash. Then, taking one of the coffee mugs, she retreated to the kitchen table. Settling into a chair, she warmed her hands on the ceramic mug as she watched Wyatt move easily around the kitchen. His dark hair was still damp from his shower, curling slightly at his nape. He had the lean build of someone who runs, and overall, he seemed fit. She remembered him mentioning a float trip on the Buffalo River, and wondered if he was a hiker. He looked outdoorsy.

He turned toward the table, plate and mug in hand, and caught her staring. "What?"

Rather than giving in to embarrassment again, she switched into interrogation mode. "Are you the outdoorsy type?"

Wyatt eyed her warily as he took the seat across from her. "Why? You planning on dropping me out in the woods with nothing but a compass and a water bottle?" He pointed the tines of his fork at her. "I have to warn you now, I don't go anywhere without a laptop and a hot spot."

She shook her head, though the image of him trudging

through the woods using his phone as a compass and with his laptop bag strapped across his chest was amusing. "I was curious. You mentioned floating the Buffalo."

"Oh." He turned his attention and his fork on the plate of food in front of him. "Yeah, sure, I like floating. I prefer a canoe to a kayak, even though I know kayaks are cooler right now. I hike the trails at Pinnacle Mountain a couple times a year, but mainly because it's so close to Little Rock and sometimes I need to get out of the office and out of my head, you know?"

"I get you," she said before taking a sip of her coffee.

Using the side of his fork, he cut the gravy-smothered biscuit into bite-size chunks. "I'm not big on camping," he said with a shrug and sheepish smile. "I'm fond of electricity."

"Me too," she assured him. "I mean, me neither." She gave a short laugh then summed it all up. "I don't camp."

"So, why are you asking if I'm 'outdoorsy' when I ask what your plan is?"

"Oh, I wasn't planning..." She laughed at the roundabout of non sequiturs they'd been riding. "Two separate trains of thought converged. Sorry."

"Ah, okay." He shoveled a bite into his mouth and chewed, closing his eyes appreciatively. After washing it down with a sip of coffee, he pulled a pained face. "I'm never going to be able to eat another frozen biscuit again."

"Ruined, huh?"

He stabbed another gravy-slathered bite but met her eyes when he answered. "Completely and utterly."

"My mama's biscuits can have an effect on a man," she cooed in an exaggerated drawl.

Wyatt only smirked as he chewed. She watched as he demolished half the plate before she spoke. "My plan is to stay here with you. Hunker down. Does your department have enough sway with Homeland Security to make it look like I boarded a flight?"

"We have sway, and we have, uh, other ways," he answered without looking up. "You want it to look like you're headed back."

"I figure it will buy us at least a day or so, and maybe a little breathing room." She wrinkled her nose. "What do you think?"

"Sounds solid. I'll loop Emma in on the plan, she'll let the others know."

"I'm going to use my phone to make a hotel reservation."

His approving expression morphed into a frown. "A hotel reservation?"

Wrapping her hands around the mug, she leaned in. "I need to make it look like I'm coming back to take care of the fire stuff. I can't stay at my house, so a hotel reservation makes sense."

"But they'll charge you for it."

Cara caught sight of the red flush creeping up his neck and opted to make light of his needless commentary. She might have money now, but it didn't mean she lost the practical frugality of a born and bred Arkansan. "I know, but I think it's important to sell whoever's watching on the notion of my imminent arrival."

He bobbed his head, but focused on his plate. "Right. Right. Good thinking."

She watched as he methodically demolished the rest of his breakfast. The moment he placed his fork on the gravy-streaked plate, she spoke up again. "There's more."

"I figured the wheels were turning." He wiped his mouth with a paper napkin, a wary gleam in his eye as he sat back. "Hit me."

"I'm going to call Chris and Tom today." Abandoning her

grip on the coffee cup, she sat up straighter. She waited as he slotted the puzzle pieces into place.

"Okay."

She inclined her head. "I know Zarah sent texts letting them know I'm okay, but I need to talk to them. We have a lot happening in the next couple weeks and I need to be in the loop."

He studied her closely, biting the inside of his cheek as he weighed her plan. The morning light streaming through the window brought out hints of gold in dark eyes fringed by unfairly thick, dark lashes. The intensity of his stare should have made her uncomfortable. But it didn't. She felt safe with him. She could trust him. And, more important, he seemed to trust her.

"What do you plan to tell them?"

"Nothing in particular," she hedged. "I want to get their thoughts on what's been happening. They're far more involved in the tech community. Chris with the investors and entrepreneurs, and Tom with the people on the tech side of things."

Wyatt raised his arms and laced his fingers behind his head. She could see the temptation to rock her mother's kitchen chair back on two legs. Watching him wrestle it into submission was amusing and more than a little endearing. She wondered if he got away with tipping his own mother's chairs back. Something told her he didn't.

"What's their response been when you've had issues before?"

She shrugged. "Obviously, we've never had anything near what's happening now. Until now all I got was the usual mix of sour grapes and good old-fashioned misogyny." Thinking back on their cavalier dismissal of the vitriol slung at her day after day made her wonder if she shouldn't have been slotting them in with the chauvinists.

As if reading her mind, he asked, "Did they take it seriously?"

"No."

The answer slipped out of her before she could give the question more than a moment's thought. But it was the truth. They didn't take the chat room slurs and vaguely threatening messages posted by anonymous commenters to heart.

But now she couldn't stop shaking all over. Someone had tried to make good on those threats. It was time for Cara to insist her partners take her contribution to the company and the threats to her safety more seriously.

"Which is why I need to talk to them now."

Chapter Twelve

Cara pulled her phone from the pocket of her hoodie and placed it on the table between them. Wyatt glanced down at the blank screen then up at her, a question in his eyes. "You want me to listen in?"

A lump rose in her throat. Unable to trust her voice, Cara simply nodded.

He eyed the phone askance. "Do they know where you are?"

She shrugged. "Maybe." When his brows drew down, she knew the time had finally come to explain how complicated her dealings with her business partners had become. "My relationship with Chris and Tom has grown…distant over the past year or so."

"Distant as in contentious?"

She shook her head, dismissing the notion a smidge too quickly. "No, I wouldn't say so," she hedged. Wyatt lowered his arms and crossed them over his chest. He didn't speak. A tactic which proved more compelling than she cared to admit. "We've grown up. Grown apart. There hasn't been a fight or anything."

What she didn't tell him was she was almost one hundred percent certain the lack of friction could be attributed to her unwillingness to engage. The truth of the matter was, she wasn't as involved in the day-to-day running of LYYF as either Chris or Tom. Until this latest onslaught of abuse, she'd simply considered their arrangement a convenient division of labor. She handled the content. Chris kept them in capital and worked publicity like a pro. And the whole house of cards was built on a platform Tom created. The collaborative efforts of the company's early days were long gone. Now, instead of pizza, beers and brainstorms, they had conference calls.

"Tell me about them," he prompted.

She raised a shoulder and let it fall. "You've probably already read most of it."

"Give it to me from your perspective."

"Chris handles the money matters. Always has. He likes wheeling and dealing. Being in the middle of the action. He bought a place in Palo Alto the minute money started coming in and moved up there to be in the center of it all. Tom stayed down in LA for a while longer, but he hated the congestion. The only things he needs to be happy are surfing, solitude and a keyboard, so he bought himself a multimillion-dollar shack near Big Sur. I stayed put."

"You never wanted to live anywhere else?"

She gave him a rueful smile. "I was still chasing fame in Hollywood, remember?"

"Then it found you on the web," Wyatt concluded. "So the three of you live and work in completely separate areas?"

She nodded. "Yes. In both the company and geographically. Which isn't an issue. We're a digital company. There's no need for us to share office space." She shrugged. "We have operations offices for the tech side of things in Mountain View, and my content team has a small production studio near me in Silver Lake."

Wyatt took a moment to process the information. His

gaze dropped to the phone again, then he asked, "Do you like your partners?"

She should have been startled by his bluntness, but Cara was becoming adept at cop speak. He was trying to catch her off guard. He didn't realize she had no reason to have her guard up. Not here. And not with him.

"I do."

The answer was simple and mostly true. Chris had grown more than a little pompous, but he'd never been lacking in the self-esteem department. Tom was surlier and more reticent with her these days, but she'd chalked it up to a natural drift. Plus, the run-up to the stock offering was forcing him out of his happy place behind a keyboard and into the spotlight. A part of her hoped they'd both revert to the easygoing guys she'd met on dormitory move-in day, but she knew it wasn't likely. She wasn't the same starry-eyed young dreamer she'd been then, either.

"Have you ever…?" he started, then stopped. She looked up at him, all too aware of what his next question would be. She'd been asked dozens of times. Still, for some reason, it nettled to know it would be coming from Wyatt. But when he spoke, his surety surprised her. "You've never been romantically involved with either of them."

She shook her head. "No. I mean, Chris hit on me once. He'd come home from a party drunk our freshman year. I didn't take it personally, though. The minute I said no, he turned his attention to another girl on our floor." She gave him a weak smile. "As far as I know, he hasn't changed much. Chris's focus has always been money. The business. Women come and they go," she explained with a dismissive wave. "I've never known him to be serious about anyone."

"And Tom?"

"Tom was as focused as Chris, but more on the nuts and

bolts. We, uh, he liked what I was doing with the meditation stuff. Tom was the one who convinced Chris to put it out there. They were light on content, and as I told you before, I was working for takeout in the early days."

"And your relationship with him never…crossed any lines?"

Her cheeks heated, but she held his gaze as she dismissed the notion. "No. I think… There was a time when I thought maybe he had feelings for me," she admitted. Gritting her teeth to ward off the blush threatening, she pushed through. "But I didn't, um, encourage him, and he never…pushed." She looked down at her hands, then chanced a peek at him from under her lashes. "I think his feelings sort of…fizzled. You know how it is. Nothing more than a crush."

"Who do you want to call first?" he prompted.

"Tom," she answered without hesitation.

Wyatt made a sort of there-it-is motion to the phone, and Cara couldn't help feeling she'd given her growing discomfiture away. Curling her lips in, she bit down gently as she took up the phone and dialed the number she'd jotted in her spiral-bound notebook. The call went directly to voicemail. When the tone sounded, she swallowed hard and did her best to keep her tone chipper. Upbeat.

"Hey, Tom. It's me. I guess Zarah has been keeping you guys up to date with what's happening with me. I, um, well, I was only checking in. Give me a call when you can," she finished, then jabbed at the red button to end the call.

"Well. Okay. Strange," she muttered under her breath.

Wyatt tapped a finger on the table to prompt her to look up at him. "Why strange?"

She exhaled long and low, her lips curving in a sad smile. "I can't remember the last time he didn't take my call."

"It's an unknown number."

She allowed her smile to grow and the blush to come. "Right. Makes sense. Logically. Feels strange though."

"Do you want to try Chris, or wait until after Tom calls you back?"

Cara caught the corner of her lip between her teeth. Staring down at the phone with its generic background and out-of-the-box ringtone, she tried to smother the unease she felt with Wyatt's confidence the call would be returned.

"I'll call him now," she said, grabbing the phone before she lost her nerve.

Once again, her call went to voicemail. She could feel Wyatt's all-consuming stare taking in every word and each morsel of nuance as she spoke. Drawing on all her years of training, Cara left the same chipper message for him, careful to say nothing more or less than she had to Tom.

When she hung up, a heavy blanket of silence fell over the room. Unable to sit still and wait, she pushed out of her chair. "More coffee?"

Wyatt declined with a shake of his head. "Your eyeballs are going to start spinning."

"I'm going to grab some water."

When she returned with two glasses filled with tinkling ice cubes, he was speaking into his own phone.

"No, I appreciate you calling me back, man," he said to the mystery caller. Mouthing an apology, he got up from the table as she reclaimed her seat, motioning his intention to take the call outside.

Cara sat at the dining table, studying the porcelain figurines her grandmother had collected for as long as Cara could remember. Her mother had helped Cara pick a new one for every birthday and Christmas Grandma June had celebrated. She'd displayed them on nearly every open surface at the old house. Now they stayed locked in a glass case, waiting for someone to take notice of them.

At times she felt like one of those Precious Moments dolls. There were days she felt her contributions to LYYF captured something innately human and essential. Other days, she wondered if she was purely decorative. She picked up her silent phone and scowled at it. The dark screen of her phone bounced her reflection back at her and she quickly altered her expression. There had been a time when she'd spent hours looking into mirrors, trying to nail the emotions with a simple shift in facial features. She could, when necessary, inject deep feeling into her tone.

Tom and Chris used to love it when she drew on her theatrical training to place their delivery or drive-through orders. "Tacos!" she'd exclaim into the speaker, breathless with desperation. "I need six tacos and a bean burrito or they'll kill me!" But LA servers were often actors or wannabe actors themselves. They rarely rose to the bait, even when she gave a performance her best friends declared Oscar-worthy.

"I called a guy I knew from the academy," Wyatt said as he strode back into the room, jolting her from her memories.

"Yeah?" she managed.

"Ryan Hastings," he said with a nod. "Worked for years on protection duty. He left the force last year to start his own security and protection firm up in Bentonville."

"Ryan Hastings," she repeated. "Why does his name sound familiar?"

"He was involved in a pretty high-profile case last year. Some big-shot attorney and his son were killed. Ryan was assigned to protect the widow. Turns out the guy's brother, a US senator, was involved."

"Yes, I remember hearing about it." She mustered a self-effacing smile. "Probably from my mother. I'm not big on absorbing the news of the world."

"It can do a number on you." Wyatt nodded. "I limit how much I take in too and try to get information from a cross section of sources."

"Wise," she affirmed.

The default ringtone on the mobile phone in front of her rang out. Cara glanced at the screen and drew in a deep breath. "It's Tom." Without looking to him for direction, she swiped to accept the call, then activated the speaker. When Wyatt sank back in his seat, she understood he meant to listen in unnoticed.

"Tom." She exhaled her old friend's name.

"Cara, are you okay? I heard about your house," he told her, sounding genuinely upset.

"Wow. It made regional coverage?" She shot Wyatt raised eyebrows. "I wouldn't have figured more than a mention on *LA Today.*"

There was a moment of hesitation on Tom's end. "Zarah sent me a link."

"Ah. Okay. Makes sense."

"She said you weren't home?"

"I wasn't."

"Any word on the damages?"

"I haven't made it back to see for myself yet, but I'm told it's all fixable."

"Thank goodness." Tom released a gusty sigh. "Where are you? Are you coming back before New York?"

When she met Wyatt's gaze, he gave an imperceptible shake of his head, but shrugged as if to say it was her call as to what to tell him.

"Zarah has booked me a flight home." Her tongue tangled on the last word. LA had been her home for years, but now it may as well have been a million miles away. An awkward beat passed in which no one spoke.

"Yeah, uh, I think she said something about you coming back when she sent the news. Sorry. You know how distracted I get."

"I do. Anyway, I should get in late tonight." Feeling disheartened by the ever-widening distance between them, she grasped for conversational straws. "When are you heading east?"

"Day after tomorrow." The dullness in his tone told her he wasn't looking forward to making the trip, even if it meant he returned to the West Coast a billionaire. "I got the files you sent for the bedtime meditation series. Good stuff."

This was about as effusive as Tom ever was about the content she provided. Usually his persona of a disengaged, flighty genius amused her, but she found she was not in the mood to be dismissed. "Should be good for another ten million or so downloads," she said, affecting the same offhanded tone.

"What?" Tom coughed, then chuckled. "Oh, yeah. At least."

Irked by the stilted conversation, she decided to introduce a whole new topic. "Hey, did you also hear some guy tried to kidnap me at gunpoint?" she asked in a mockingly bright tone. "With a real gun and everything. Guess you can believe some of the stuff you read on the forums after all."

"Cara, I'm so sorry about what happened," he said in a rush of words. "I mean, you know I'm happy you're okay. I'd hate for you to get hurt—"

His verbal stumbling and bumbling only angered her more. He'd never been the most socially adroit guy, but this was beyond ridiculous.

"Can't kill the cash cow." She smiled as she said it, but a cold knot formed in her belly. Needing to end this torture, she leaned in, her face close to the phone. "I'll see you in New York, Tom. Safe travels." She ended the call with an angry jab of her forefinger.

When she looked up, she found Wyatt staring at her, brows raised. "And he's the one you're closer to?"

"He's…Tom. His mind is always miles down the road, you know?" She took a steadying breath. "I'm mostly used to it, but sometimes it would be nice if he could at least try living in the present."

Wyatt nodded. "There's this great meditation app I use…"

She gave an appreciative chuckle. "When he said the files I sent for the new series are good, I can guarantee he was talking about the audio quality, not the content." The corner of her mouth kicked up in a smirk. "Tom considers sleep a waste of productive hours."

"But Chris has to know content is king," Wyatt argued. "I mean, he's the guy out there pushing for investors and users, right?"

"Oh, yeah. Chris likes to say I'm the best impulse buy he's ever made."

"Whoa." Wyatt blinked and fell back in his chair. "Please tell me he's joking."

"I'd say it's about eighty-five percent joke," she conceded.

His brows drew down. "Do you ever think about leaving? Selling out and going off to do whatever you want to do?"

"Sure, I think about it." She shrugged. "The question is, what would I do? Actresses have a much narrower window when it comes to breaking into the business. Mine's pretty much closed. There's off-screen work, but there my success with LYYF may work against me."

"How?"

"Well, my voice is fairly recognizable now." She gave him a wan smile. "Having a familiar voice can be an advantage for men—look at Matthew McConaughey, Morgan Freeman or James Earl Jones. But women doing voice-over work? Sure, you get the occasional celebrities pushing perfume at Christmastime, or splash-washing their fully made-up faces for some beauty brand, but they're mainly hired for the on-camera work, not to be the voice of the product."

"And you're already inherently entwined with another brand," he said with grim understanding.

"Exactly."

She was saved from further discussion of her personal and professional choices by the buzzing of her phone. A peek at the display showed Chris's number. She smiled grimly and stretched a hand out to accept the call. "And now contestant number two."

She swiped the screen and called out, "Hey, Chris," before Wyatt even straightened in his chair.

"Cara, holy cripes," her longtime business partner gushed. "I'm so glad you called. I've been worried sick ever since Zarah told me what happened."

"What happened a couple days ago, or what happened last night?" Cara prodded.

"Last night? What happened last night?"

She looked up and met Wyatt's eyes. Chris sounded truly perplexed.

"Someone set my house on fire."

"The house where you're staying in Alabama?" he asked, sounding genuinely aghast.

She and Wyatt shared an amused smirk. "Arkansas. And no. I meant my house in LA," she corrected.

"No way! The little place in Los Feliz?"

"Yes." She leaned in closer. "You hadn't heard? I thought maybe Zarah—"

"Oh, she may have," he interrupted. "I've been running all

over New York taking meeting after meeting," he said in a rush. "But you weren't there, right? You're in, uh, Arkansas?"

"Zarah booked me on a flight to LAX this evening." She held Wyatt's stare but said no more.

"Hey, Cara, you think you might consider hiring some security," Chris suggested. "At least until all this stuff blows over. I think we may have been a bit…"

In her mind, Cara filled the empty air space with a few choice adjectives: *condescending…dismissive*?

"I mean, you never know when to take the trolls seriously. Am I right?"

"Right," she replied flatly.

She stared at the phone screen, wishing they were on a video call. It was hard to get a read on this version of Chris. She'd grown so used to thinking of him as little more than her business partner. She'd almost forgotten they were once good friends.

"So, yeah, maybe it's time for us to be more proactive about security. For you, and maybe all three of us?"

Cara couldn't remember the last time Chris's innate confidence had seemed so shaken. Now she wished she could have her old cavalier Chris back. His obvious worry made her feel all the more exposed. Picking up the pen Wyatt abandoned, she twirled it through her fingers like a baton.

"Maybe. I'll look into it," she promised, her gaze darting back up to Wyatt.

"Let me know how things are when you get back to LA," Chris insisted. "When are you coming east?"

Not wanting to be pinned down to anything resembling a schedule, she kept her answer as vague as possible. "I'll be there a day or two before to do any media you want me to handle and will probably beat a path out of there right after. You know I'm not a New York girl."

"Some actor you are," he teased, echoing an old refrain. "Aren't you all supposed to claim to want to have a serious stage career?"

"Not me," she answered, trying to muster some of her old bravado as she tossed out the line he expected from her. "I never said I wanted to be an actress. I want to be a star."

"You are a star," Chris replied. "The investors love you. We all do. Be careful and I'll see you next week."

Three long beeps sounded to indicate the end of the call. She pressed her lips together to stave off an unexpected rush of emotion. Dropping the pen to the table with a clatter, she pushed back and escaped the dining room before Wyatt could get a word out. She didn't know what to say anymore. Everything seemed to be the opposite of what it should be.

Roscoe lifted his big, square head and let out a soft woof when she pushed through the screen door onto the porch. She stood at the rail, her arms crossed tight across her chest, staring out at the spot where the old house once stood. Her jaw clenched tight, she shivered when the crisp autumn breeze cut through the cotton sweatshirt she wore. Tugging the sleeves down over her hands, she scowled down at the discount store athletic wear. Why hadn't Zarah included some regular clothes? Did she think Cara would be practicing sun salutations and Savasana while on the run from her tormentors?

Cara clamped down on her uncharitable thoughts, her fingers biting into the thin cotton fabric as she hugged herself again. Zarah had done her best. She'd found clothing and other necessities at a store with delivery while sitting in her snug home office over a thousand miles away. She should be grateful for the ease and comfort of the clothing. For her safety. She should be happy there were other people who were glad she was alive. And she was.

"Cara?"

The quiet, husky timbre of Wyatt's voice sent a different sort of shiver through her. Roscoe, who'd settled back in his customary repose, did little more than open an eye. Her cheeks flamed as she heard the hinges on the screen door squeak. She didn't dare turn to look at him.

"You want me to grab one of your mom's jackets?"

"I'm okay."

She clearly wasn't. Cara could almost feel him struggling to suppress the urge to argue the point. But to his credit, he retreated, the hinges creaking again. "How about I put on a fresh pot of coffee?"

A sob rose in her throat. Cara bludgeoned the knot of emotion with a short, sharp laugh. "I thought you were worried about spinning eyeballs."

"I'm a cop. I'm trained to withstand torturous levels of overcaffeination. I was worried about your eyeballs."

She turned to look at him, hoping he'd assume the color in her cheeks came courtesy of the wind. "Thank you. I wasn't quite up to my eyeballs yet, but didn't want you to feel emasculated."

"I appreciate your concern," he intoned gravely. He reached out to the side, pulled a fleece-lined denim jacket from the hall tree and popped the screen door open wide enough to thrust it at her. "I'll be in the kitchen when you're ready to talk."

She gave herself no more than five minutes to stew, sulk and otherwise sort through the swirl of conflicting emotions before she headed back into the house. Roscoe opted to relinquish his sunny spot in favor of shelter as well. She shrugged out of the jacket and hung it on its customary hook before following the old dog to the kitchen.

Wyatt was measuring grounds into the basket when she entered the room. Rather than jumping in to help him, Cara stopped at the table and watched. His movements were economical, but fluid. Almost graceful. He was comfortable moving around her parents' kitchen. She'd never pictured herself bringing a man home. Not that she'd brought him there in any sort of romantic way. But she'd never pictured it at all.

She'd never invited Chris or Tom to accompany her on trips home. Like most people from the coast, they considered anyplace west of Philadelphia akin to traveling to the outback. Tom had been offered an obscene amount of money to speak at a prestigious convention in Chicago and refused. To her partners, the middle of the country was an unappealing wilderness filled with dangerous creatures and backward people.

As Wyatt poured water into the coffee maker's reservoir, she felt an unexpected twist of sympathy for them. They would never know the pleasure of waking to the scent of strong black coffee and fresh-baked biscuits. They'd never know what a relief it was to have conversations with people who spoke slowly, choosing their words with thought and ending their sentences declaratively, rather than as questions. And there was no doubt in her mind which rock they needed to kick over next.

She gripped the back of her father's chair. "I think you're right. We need to take a closer look at Chris and Tom."

Wyatt stilled for a moment, then reached for the dishcloth hanging beside the sink to wipe his hands. When he turned to face her, his eyes were full of sympathy and a familiar resolve. "Ryan Hastings said the same thing. He says the threat almost always stems from a source close to the vic— uh, person of interest."

She gave him a wan smirk. "Thanks for not calling me a victim."

"You aren't one." He pulled a coffee mug closer. "Maybe we need to look at Zarah too."

Cara shrugged. "She doesn't have anything to gain from getting rid of me, though."

"True." He hit the button to start the coffee brewing, then gestured to the kitchen table. "But she seems to be in the middle of everything."

Cara conceded the point. It seemed more and more of her communication with her partners ran through Zarah these days.

Wyatt nodded. "We'll start with a brain dump of everything you can come up with concerning your partners." He hung the towel back on the hook, then fixed her with a look. "I asked Emma to rebook your flight for morning. If anyone asks, you can say you couldn't make the drive to Little Rock on time. Either way, it'll buy us a little more time on the going-to-California story."

"Good call." She nodded, impressed.

"I'd have handled it myself, but I couldn't be sure the connection would be there. I've crashed and burned more since we've been here than any time since I was in high school," he said with a grimace.

Cara laughed. "I'm sorry. And I have to say, I doubt you crashed and burned much in high school or since."

"Thanks, but either way, tomorrow we're driving into town to get a 5G gateway. I can't rough it with this faulty connection any longer."

Cara hid her smile as she moved to pull a fresh mug from the cupboard. Apparently, even the most down-to-earth men needed their creature comforts. "Sounds good." And it did. As good as it was to feel safe and secure on the ranch, she was starting to feel restless. It would be good to get out for a little while.

Chapter Thirteen

The following morning, the two of them drove north in search of a more reliable source of internet access. It was clear that if Wyatt was going to dig into the financials of three tech titans, he was going to need more speed than the spotty satellite could provide.

They rode in companionable silence, sipping coffee as they wound their way into Boone County. Wyatt glanced over at Cara as they approached the outskirts of Harrison, the next town of any size along the highway. "I should be able to get what I need at any cellular store, but if they don't have one in stock, we may need to head up to Branson or Springfield."

She shrugged. "Fine with me. My calendar is open all day."

"We can pick up anything else you might need while we're here," he offered.

She plucked at the front of her hoodie. Leaning against the door, she turned toward him. "My mom used to take me into Harrison to do my school clothes shopping. I didn't realize people bought clothes anywhere but JCPenney until I was about eleven and discovered the joys of a store called Goody's. They had all the cool stuff."

"My mom liked to drive up to North Little Rock so she could wander around the mall."

"Lucky you, shopping in the big city."

He rolled his eyes.

They crested one of the rolling hills and Cara's phone sprang to life with a series of texts from Zarah coming through in rapid succession.

Zarah: I went to pick you up and you weren't on the plane.

Zarah: Checked and saw you rebooked for AM. Hope all is okay.

Zarah: You're not answering my messages. Hot cop got your phone?

Her cheeks flamed as she read the last one, knowing at some point Wyatt would see it and know there'd been speculation about him. She was trying to formulate a response when a new message appeared.

Zarah: I'm picking you up at the airport. Hope you made your flight. Text when you land.

"Oh, crud," Cara muttered.

"What's the matter?"

"Zarah's waiting for my flight at LAX," she reported. She typed a response, then quickly deleted it. "You said Emma could do something to make it look like I got on the flight, right?"

Wyatt frowned. "Yeah. Why?"

"Zarah never picks me up from the airport. She lives on the other end of the earth," she mumbled, scowling at her phone.

"Hang tight." Eyeing a gas station ahead on the highway, Wyatt signaled his intention to pull over. Once he'd pulled into a parking spot outside a bustling mini-mart, he turned to look at Cara. "Tell me all about Zarah."

Her eyebrows shot up. "All about Zarah?" she repeated, punctuating the request with an incredulous scoff. "Where do I begin?"

"How did you meet her?" he prompted.

"Well, I hired her long before I actually met her," she said slowly. "It was at the start of the pandemic lockdown, and we couldn't turn out content fast enough."

Wyatt unhooked his seat belt and turned to look at her. "So your relationship has always been remote?"

"Yes. I mean, we've met since then, obviously," she said with a helpless wave of her hand. "But we've never shared office space. A lot of LYYF's staff works remotely."

"How did she come to work for you?"

"One of the programmers," she said with a frown. "They are cousins or something?" She brushed the fuzzy details aside. "Anyway, she was doing some travel booking for Tom, and then Chris. When we opened the offices in Mountain View, Chris and Tom took offices there and they have someone on-site. Being based in Southern California, it only made sense for Zarah to focus more on me."

"But she doesn't do stuff for you in person," he clarified.

"No. She didn't even want a desk at the production studio." She shrugged. "Like I said, she lives out in the Valley. It doesn't seem like a long way away when you look at a map, but when you factor in LA traffic…"

"And the airport?" Wyatt asked, making a winding gesture with his hand.

"Is even farther."

"Can you try to find out why she's picking you up? You know, subtly?" he asked, looking troubled. "Without giving away anything about where you are?"

She rolled her eyes. "Gee, I don't know," she drawled, settling into her seat. She typed out a message with her thumbs but before she hit Send, she turned the screen to him for approval.

CB: You're sweet, but it's too far away. Don't worry about me.

"Perfect," Wyatt said with a nod.

She sent the message and let out a long sigh.

The silence stretched taut between them. Finally, he broke it. "What are you thinking?"

She mustered a small, sad smile. "I'm thinking maybe I should give them all what they want."

"Who? And what?" he asked cautiously.

"Everyone. No one thinks I deserve my thirty-three-and-a-third of LYYF. Maybe I should sell out and go do something new. I mean, it's not like I wouldn't have options. I'd certainly have the money to coast for a while."

"Wait until after next week and you'd probably have the money to coast forever," he pointed out.

"Ah, but they don't think I've earned a big payday. People aren't assaulting innocent neighbors and burning down my house because they're hoping I sell after the stock offering. They want me out now. And what does it matter? Either way, I'll have more money than I need."

"What if selling isn't enough? From what I've seen and read, some people think you should be paying LYYF for the pleasure of putting together their award-winning content." He gave a little snort. "No. Don't sell out because they—whoever they are—want you to. If you want out, make sure you leave on your terms."

Her phone buzzed and she looked down. Another message from Zarah had arrived.

Zarah: It's no problem. See you soon.

"I have a feeling she knows I'm not on the plane," Cara said, her tone morose.

"Okay, so tell her." He gestured to the phone. "Let her know you talked to the LAFD and they said there was no reason to hurry back so you changed your mind."

"Tell her I stayed in Arkansas?" she asked, her forehead knit with concern. "What if someone's reading our texts?"

"You can make it sound like you decided to head to New York early. Might be the better idea," he added. "Let them try to find the needle in the haystack there."

Cara set her jaw. At last, she nodded and began to type.

CB: So sorry. Spoke to LAFD and they said no need to hurry back. Canceled flight. I'll deal with the house after the IPO. Probably head to NYC early. Go home. I appreciate the thought!

Then she turned the phone off and tossed it into the console. She caught his quizzical look and pulled a face.

"I'm starting to think all this technology is more trouble than it's worth." He chuckled and her expression brightened. "We could blow off getting your hot spot thingy. You know those phone places like to keep you trapped all day, and I know a place with the best onion rings you've ever tasted."

He let out a guffaw as he pulled his seat belt across his body and clicked it into place. "It's nine thirty and we finished breakfast less than an hour ago."

"I fail to see the conflict," she replied, straight-faced.

"How does this sound? I grab the gateway—it won't take long, the state has a contract with the carrier and it's all set up at the store." He sneaked a glance at her as he maneuvered out of the cramped parking lot. *Skeptical* wasn't a strong enough word for the look she gave him. "Seriously. All I have to do is show my ID and pick it up." She shot him a doubtful glance as he pulled back onto the highway.

"Fine," she conceded ungraciously.

"Then we can see what we can do about finding you some different clothes. You brought the cash Zarah sent?" She nodded and gave an affirmative hmm. "Good." He smiled as they picked up speed, hurtling toward the small city nestled in the Ozark Mountains. "Then we'll replenish with those onion rings, but I have to warn you, I've had some good rings in my time."

"In your time," she echoed with a snort.

He drummed his fingers on the steering wheel, smiling as he glanced over at her. "So tell me, who is this hot cop Zarah asked you about?"

THE PICKUP AT the mobile phone store didn't go as quickly or smoothly as Wyatt had hoped. When all was said and done, it ate through a full hour of their morning and layers of his patience.

"Come on, we'll get a ridiculously decadent cup of coffee, then I'll let you sit and watch the world go by while I try on jeans and pick up a few sweaters." She treated him to a wide, winning smile. "I've lived in Southern California for so long I've forgotten how great sweater weather actually is."

As they waited at the window to pick up overpriced coffees, Cara leaned across him to ask the young woman at the register for shopping recommendations. When he ruled out a trip to the Branson outlets, she insisted he drive her to the town square. Wyatt eyed the area skeptically. Like most small towns, Harrison had dried up when the highway bypass was built and commerce flowed away from the business district.

"There it is." Cara pointed to one of the run-down store-fronts. "Sassafras," she announced, repeating the name of the boutique the woman at the coffee shop said had "real cute stuff" but was "kinda spendy."

The display window featured a single mannequin sporting a pair of slim black pants and an animal-print sweater with an enormous collar pulled down around its sculpted shoulders. Wyatt tried to picture Cara wearing such an outland-ishly gaudy print but found he could imagine the tempting hollows of her collarbones all too easily.

"Maybe we should go up to Branson," he said gruffly.

She let out a tinkling burst of laughter. "Maybe, but I'll take a peek in here first."

When she reached for the handle, he placed a hand on her forearm to stop her. "Hang on. Let me go in and check it out first."

Raising a single brow, she asked, "You think whoever is stalking me somehow got wind of a random conversation I had with a barista through a drive-up window?"

"No," he admitted slowly. "But I'm, uh, responsible for, you know, keeping you safe."

The other brow shot up to match its twin. "Well, come on, Captain Responsible, we're going shopping. You can hold my keeper pile."

She bailed out of the SUV without another word and Wyatt cringed at the thought. He could have handled a trip to a mall. Department stores usually had chairs for people to wait in, at least. But this place looked to be about the size of a postage stamp and, from what he could see through the plate-glass door, was stuffed to the gills with glitter, fringe and frills. When Cara stopped on the sidewalk, crossed her arms over her chest and tapped her foot, he made a shooing motion before opening his own door.

"Go on. I'm getting claustrophobic lookin' through the window," he called to her.

Cara's triumphant grin lit her face. "I won't be long," she called, then sailed into the store without a backward glance.

He heard the jingle of the bell above the store's door as he climbed out of the car himself. Carrying his coffee, he strolled along the sidewalk, peering around the edges of brown-craft-papered windows into vacant spaces, and stopping to admire the neon marquee of the historic Lyric Theater. Not wanting to stray too far, he settled on a wooden park bench across from Sassafras. He'd responded to three work emails and was sipping the dregs of his coffee when she backed out of the store, shopping bags pulling on both arms.

The yoga pants, T-shirt and sweatshirt she'd been wearing were nowhere to be found. Instead, she wore wide-legged bleached denim jeans with a preppy-looking sweater. She still wore the thick-soled canvas sneakers Zarah had sent with the other supplies, but he could see the distinct shape of a shoebox in one of the bulging bags. Tossing his cup into a nearby trash bin, he hustled to the car to help her stow her haul.

"Wow. I guess this worked for you?" he asked with a laugh.

"Such cute stuff. Fun but functional. They have a whole

section of jeans called 'sassy pants,'" she informed him as he pried the handles of the shoppers from her fingers.

"I would expect nothing less," he said soberly.

"I'm going to tell my mom about this place. She'd love it too," she called as she headed for the passenger seat.

Wyatt had a hard time imagining practical, efficient Betsy Beckett shopping anywhere with so much sass, but he refrained from saying so. When he climbed back into the driver's seat, he could practically feel the buzz emanating from her. Her excitement was so infectious, he had to smile.

"I guess you needed some retail therapy?"

"I needed to make some of my own choices," she countered without missing a beat. She looked over at him. "I've been wearing clothes someone else picked out, sleeping in a bed I haven't felt comfortable in since I was seventeen, riding around in a car I don't own, with a guy I barely know, and eating random vegetables scrounged from the depths of my parents' deep freeze." She flashed a shaky smile. "I'm pretty sure there are jars of pickles in the cellar older than I am."

Wyatt blew out a breath, his shoulders drooping as he took in her words. "Man, Cara, I'm sorry—"

"No." She held up a hand, cutting him off. "I'm grateful. For all of it. Grateful I got away from Gerald Griffin, grateful to have friends and financial wherewithal to do this. Not everyone has a soft place to land…a place to call home no matter how long they've been away. I'm so lucky and I know it," she said earnestly. "But today, I needed a few minutes to just be me, you know?"

"I get it."

"It feels like all I've been doing for the past few weeks is reacting." She looked him directly in the eye. "Honestly, I don't know how much longer I can do this. I can't live my life according to rules other people make up for me."

"I understand."

And he did. Wyatt knew he'd be champing at the bit if he were in her shoes. Shock and sheer terror had carried her for days. She'd bounced from one blow to the next like a boxer pinned against the ropes.

But now she was coming around.

This punch-drunk powerhouse outfitted in her brand-new sassy pants would soon be ready to come out swinging, and he was going to be the guy to hold whoever was responsible for terrorizing her up for her to pummel.

She reached for her abandoned cup of coffee and took a healthy slug. She wrinkled her nose as she dropped it back into the cup holder. "Not so tempting when it's tepid."

"We can get a fresh one for the ride home," he offered, reversing out of the parking space.

"Nah, I promised you lunch, remember?"

"I rarely forget about onion rings," he intoned gravely.

She jiggled her knee, clearly still hyped up on her taste of freedom. "Excellent. Head out to Highway 7 South. There's a dairy bar down the road a piece."

"I love a good dairy bar." He hit his turn signal and headed in the direction she indicated.

A few miles outside town, Cara contented herself with an order of hand-battered onion rings while he wolfed down a ridiculously sloppy barbecue bacon burger the woman at the order window claimed was the best thing on the chalkboard menu.

Cara crunched into a ring the circumference of a softball and hummed her appreciation as she chewed, her gaze fixed on a point in the middle distance.

"Everything okay?" It was a ridiculous question, given their circumstances, but he was dying to know where her mind was.

"Do you mind if we stop by a grocery store on our way back through town?"

The request jarred a laugh from him. "Worried about your next meal already?"

"Always," she replied without missing a beat. "I was thinking I could pick up some fruit besides apples and oranges, and I'd sell an internal organ for a bean burrito."

"Wow. Quite a refined palate you have there. I'm not sure your internal organs would fetch a good price on the open market if all you're eating are bean burritos."

"Oh, I eat other things. Given something other than plastic-wrapped American cheese slices, I can put together a grilled cheese sandwich deserving a Michelin star," she boasted.

"I believe all grilled cheese sandwiches deserve a Michelin star, but you can be snobby if it makes you feel better."

"Some feta, nuts and quinoa would make me feel much better about eating the bagged salads my mom bought me." She took a noisy slurp of the chocolate milkshake she'd ordered, then let her head fall back against the seat. "And I could get some Brussels sprouts to grill."

He shuddered then reached over to swipe an onion ring from the paper bag. "I can't believe you're even thinking about Brussels sprouts while eating these."

"What can I say? I'm multidimensional," she said, gesturing for him to finish the last ring off. "And I can't go on eating potatoes, onions and okra. I'm going to turn into gumbo."

"Well, we can't have that." He crumpled his own wrapper, gathered their trash and reached for the door handle. "I'll go toss this and we'll be on our way. We need to get back. I have work to do."

While Cara shopped, Wyatt called her parents to let them

know they were in town longer than expected, but the call went to voicemail. Forty minutes later, they were sailing down Highway 65 hauling a decent sampling from Cara's favorite food groups—cheese, frozen burritos, snack crackers and breakfast pastries.

"Why don't you try calling your parents? Let them know we're heading back," he suggested, nodding to the phone she'd tossed into the console on their way into town.

"Dad said he needed to replace some wire on the western fence," she said as she powered the phone on. "Mom's probably helping him."

Wyatt frowned. "I could have helped him."

Cara glanced over at him, a faintly amused smile tugging at her lips. "You think my mom doesn't know how to stretch fence?"

"I think your mom can do anything," he replied without missing a beat. "I'm only saying I would have been happy to help."

"And I'm sure they'd appreciate the offer, but they know you're here on other business."

She jolted and they both looked down as the phone in her hand emitted several short bursts of vibration. "Someone was looking for you," he said grimly. "Was it your folks?"

Cara's lips thinned into a tight line. "No."

She snapped the word off so sharply, he checked her again. "Do I need to pull over?"

"It's nothing. More text messages from my biggest fans," she said, her voice tight with bitterness.

He reached over and took the phone from her hand. A quick glance showed a string of text messages from a variety of area codes. A surge of anger pulsed through him. He wanted to pull over to read them, but the stretch of road they were on had little to offer in terms of a shoulder. So he opted for the second-best thing. He pressed and held the power button as he maneuvered a curve one-handed.

"What did they say?" he demanded in a growl.

"I only saw the notification windows, but they looked to be more of the same. I don't deserve my share of LYYF. I should leave the company to the real geniuses. Blah blah blah," she muttered, turning to look out on a broad swatch of pastureland. "I'm so tired of it all," she whispered.

Without thinking, he dropped the phone back into the console and reached across to place a steadying hand on her leg. The moment his palm landed she tensed and he froze for a beat. Then he jerked his arm back, gripping the steering wheel like a fifteen-year-old angling for a learner's permit.

"Sorry," he breathed. "I didn't mean—"

"It's okay," she said, trampling his apology. "And I know. I appreciate you being here. I appreciate everything you're doing, Wyatt." She angled to look directly at him. "I hope you know I do."

"I do."

A horn blared and he glanced up into the rearview mirror. "Holy cow, this guy needs to slow down," he muttered, inching the SUV to the right as a sleek silver sports car swerved into oncoming traffic to pass. "Double yellow, dude," Wyatt complained, gesturing to the markings on the road.

"Missouri plates," Cara observed as the car dropped back into the lane in front of them.

The driver immediately ran up on the bumper of the next car ahead of them. The coupe was so low-slung the driver was barely visible over the headrest. Cara gripped the door handle. Wyatt tightened his hands on the wheel, half-expecting to witness a terrible accident as the erratic driver overtook car after car, heedless of the rules of the road.

"Wanna throw your cop light up onto the roof and go after them like on TV?"

He shot her a wry smile but kept their speed steady as the other car disappeared over a hill. "Sadly, this ride didn't come equipped with a cop light."

"So sad."

Wyatt shook his head in wonder as the line of traffic shaken by the aggressive driving of the speeder settled into a more sedate pace.

They rode in silence for a couple miles. Then turning her attention back to the road, she pointed to a blur of a highway sign. "If you turn off on 14, we can come in the back side. It's hilly and curvy, but it's a pretty drive and we could check to see if Mama and Daddy are in the west pasture on our way to the house."

"Sounds good."

They drove into the small town of St. Joe in tight silence. The *click-click* of the turn signal sounded almost laughably loud to his own ears. Ryan Hastings's warnings about getting too attached to a primary while on protection duty reverberated in his brain. Then again, Ryan knew the dangers firsthand. He'd fallen for Kayla Powers while trying to protect her from a murderer, given up his career with the state police and moved to Bentonville to help her raise the baby she hadn't known was on the way at the time of her late husband's death.

"Cara, I shouldn't have—"

"Please don't, Wyatt," she cut him off, the words quiet but firm. She reached over and placed her hand on his arm. "I don't want things to be awkward between us. I feel… Can't we…?" She stumbled to a stop as he slowed to make the turn onto the narrow secondary road. "I didn't mind. Okay? It's… Wow, things are complicated right now, and I don't—"

"You don't have to say anything more," he interrupted.

"Well, it seems like one of us does," she countered. "Sheesh, I mean…how 'bout them Hogs?"

He laughed, amused by her use of a native's shorthand for, *Let's change the subject, please.*

"How about those Hogs?" He smiled and let off the gas as they wound through a series of curves. "I don't know if they'll make it to a bowl game this year or not."

"You realize I have absolutely no idea how the Razorbacks are doing this year, don't you?"

"I do, but I'm willing to roll with it if you are."

"Okay then. Give me the midseason highlights," she invited. "It is midseason, right? I think I remember football going until Thanksgiving."

"You aren't far off," he said encouragingly. "Okay, here's where we are."

He spent a good fifteen minutes giving her the rundown on how the University of Arkansas football team was performing, who their star players were, and a fairly in-depth analysis on the current coaching staff. For her part, Cara pretended to listen, interjecting the occasional hums and snorts where his commentary warranted response. He was about to launch into his views on the ongoing college athletic conference realignments when she held up a hand.

"Okay, uncle," she cried.

He glanced over and found her smiling at him, her eyes crinkling at the corners. He grinned back at her. "Bet you never pull the old 'How 'bout them Hogs?' on a guy again," he teased.

"Are you kidding me? I've been using that line to distract my father since I was trying to get around his no-dating-before-sixteen rule," she said with a smug smile. "Turn left up here, then we'll take a quick right on the farm road."

He did as instructed. A quarter mile down the dirt road, they came to the section of missing fence Jim had pointed out to him on their tour of the property. The ATV Jim used was parked near the opening. He could see the coils of new wire to be stretched in the bed of the utility vehicle, but Jim and Betsy Beckett were nowhere in sight.

A set of deep ruts was cut into the ground from the edge of the road, the far side of the ditch and through the gap in the fence. Either one of the Becketts had driven the farm truck out to the pasture, or someone had come to call.

Slowing to a stop, he reached for his cell phone, but Cara had beaten him to it.

Her mother answered on the second ring. "Cara, honey, is that you?" Betsy asked, her voice tremulous.

"Mama? Where are you? Where's Daddy?" Cara asked, panic rising in her voice.

"Why, we're up at the house, sweetheart," Betsy cooed, her tone a shade too bright. "Are you almost to Little Rock? You don't want to miss your flight again, sugar. I know you think you have more money than God, but those tickets are expensive," she added with a tittering laugh.

"Mama? What's happening?" Cara demanded.

"Nothin' happening here. Paul Stanton stopped by for a visit. You remember Mr. Stanton? I guess I should say Lieutenant Governor Stanton." Her mother gave a high-pitched giggle and the hairs at Wyatt's nape rippled. "He's so sad he missed seeing you. But listen, I'm bein' rude," she said, her drawl thickening in her rush. "You get on now, and be sure to call us and tell us when you've landed safely. Love you, honey. Your daddy and I love you so very much."

The call ended.

Cara turned to look at him wide-eyed. "She's acting like we're on our way to Little Rock to catch a flight."

He shook his head. "She knows we're not, but whoever is there with her doesn't." He scowled. "Paul Stanton is there? The lieutenant governor?"

She bobbed her head. "Mama went to prom with him back in the day, but Daddy hates the guy. Wyatt, something weird is going on."

"I gathered as much," he said gruffly. "But I have to get you away from here."

"I can't go off and leave them," she argued, shrugging out of her seat belt.

"You can't go in there. Not with whatever is happening," he shot back.

"Those are my parents," she said, agitation pitching her voice high and tight.

"I'm aware, but—"

The next thing he knew, the passenger door was hanging wide open and Cara was leaping across the ditch. He shouted after her, but she didn't look back. He was still fumbling with the clip on his seat belt when he heard the engine on the ATV turn over.

She took off like a shot, careening over the bumpy hill at the edge of the property, headed straight for the house. Cursing under his breath, he lunged across the seat and grappled for the handle on the open door. The moment it was closed, he threw the car into gear and cranked the wheel. The SUV hit the bottom of the ditch so hard his head smacked the roof. He aimed for the opening in the fence, squeezing his eyes shut as he plowed through, a piece of the broken fencing scraping the length of the passenger door.

He couldn't think about damage to the state-owned vehicle now.

He had to catch up with a woman who preached the gospel of staying in the moment, but was proving to be an expert at making a quick getaway.

Chapter Fourteen

Cara spotted the enormous luxury SUV parked in the drive from a quarter mile out. She fixed her sights on it, opening up the throttle and clenching her jaw to keep from clacking her teeth on every rut and ridge hidden beneath browning grass and fallen leaves.

Paul Stanton. Paul Stanton. She'd known the man all her days, but for the life of her, she could not form a picture of him. Brown hair—probably grayish brown now. Brown eyes? Probably. Her overriding recollection of the man was he was bland. Handsome enough in a conventional way.

Neat. For some reason, she recalled shirts pressed to a crisp, khaki pants with knife-edge pleats and loafers polished to a high gloss. In other words, the polar opposite of her ruggedly handsome if not a bit rumpled and work-worn father.

It was no wonder her mother had dumped Mr. Permanent Pressed for her father.

"Gah!" she cried when she hit a bump so hard the rear of the gator skittered to the side. She let off the gas until she regained control, then hit it again the moment she felt all four wheels were under her.

The pearly white SUV parked behind her father's mud-spattered pickup gleamed in the afternoon sunlight. She squinted when the shining chrome trim tossed sunlight back at her. She took pleasure in skidding to a stop right beside the hulking vehicle, sending up a plume of dust and gravel she hoped marred the sparkling paint job.

She killed the engine and leaped from the ATV. She was skirting the back of Paul Stanton's vehicle when she slid to an abrupt stop. Parked beside the massive car was another. This one low-slung and sleek. A matte silver with an all-too-familiar profile. Hurrying to the rear of the sports car, she knew what she would find.

Missouri plates.

The driver who'd been in such a hurry on the highway had been swerving in and out of traffic, endangering the lives of other drivers so he could get here faster.

Here. To her parents' little ranch in the Ozarks. Her safe haven. The place she could hide out without anyone knowing where she was. No one except Paul Stanton.

Cara reached into the back pocket of her jeans for her phone but came up empty.

Cringing, she darted a glance at the field she'd sped across to get to them. She had no doubt Wyatt would be hot on her heels, but he would have to come around via the farm and county roads. She couldn't wait for him. Wouldn't. She was the one who'd brought this madness to her mother and father's doorstep. She would be the one to stop it.

Rolling her shoulders back, she circled the corner of the house and came up the front walk. Only then did she register the steady stream of gruff, rhythmic barks. Roscoe, bless him, was standing at attention, his forehead furrowed with concern and the hair on his back standing on end, barking to be let inside to inspect the newcomers.

Walking softly, Cara crooned the old dog's name as she climbed the shallow steps. She scratched behind his floppy ears, then pressed her forehead to his to calm him. "Who's in there, boy? Bad guys? Guys with bad hair? Why was Mama talking all funny, huh?"

The dog sat at her feet, his hindquarters hitting the deck with a thump.

"Don't worry. I'll get 'em. You stay here and tell Wyatt where we're at, okay?"

Creeping off the porch, she circled around to the kitchen door. Her mother had hung sheets out to dry in the sun. Cara pictured the state-of-the-art washer-dryer set in the laundry room sitting idle while Betsy Beckett's linens snapped in the autumn breeze. She could make out the muffled hum of conversation coming from the kitchen, but was too short to catch a peek through the window over the sink.

As quietly as she could, she took the two steps up the back stoop and pressed the button on the screen-door handle.

The click of the latch opening might as well have been a shotgun blast.

Cara froze, tensing every muscle in her body. She listened intently, but no one inside spoke. She bit the inside of her cheek, figuring she'd give it to the count of five before she proceeded.

She only made it to three.

"Well, hello there, Cara."

She looked up to find Paul Stanton smiling down at her beneficently from the screened back porch. He looked incongruous standing there next to the chest freezer, amid a jumble of discarded boots, rain and cold weather gear and the motley collection of half-dead houseplants her mother refused to give up on entirely.

The man who greeted her lived up to her recollections. His hair was indeed brown, but the close-cropped helmet now sported sleek silvery sidewalls. The buttons on his starched shirt strained across a round drum of a belly. He smiled down at her, but no warmth reached his dark eyes.

"Your mama was under the impression you were headin' down to Little Rock to catch a flight, but my friend couldn't locate any information about a flight booked, so we thought we'd hang around a bit to see if maybe you'd changed your mind. Again." He pressed the flat of his palm to the screen door, and she stumbled back a step as it swung open. "Come on in. We've been waiting for you to get home."

She took two steps back, her sneakered feet crunching the leaves gathered along the side of the porch. "Who's we?"

He flashed a wide politician's smile. "Why don't you come in and we'll all chat a bit. Your mama has poured us all a glass of her delicious sweet tea."

Riled by his ingratiating tone, she stood her ground. "Who? What friend? What are you doing here?"

"We came to talk to you, is all. From what I hear, you can be a very difficult young lady to pin down."

"Cara, honey, you go on," her mother called from inside the house. "I don't want you to miss— Oh!"

The surprise and distress Cara heard in her mother's sharp cry set her in motion. Running up the steps, she brushed past Paul Stanton and his smarmy smile and charged into the kitchen. "Mama!"

Three steps into the room she drew up short. Zarah Parvich was standing in her parents' kitchen, her feet planted wide and her expression disconcertingly businesslike as she pressed the muzzle of a gun to Cara's father's temple. "Hello, Cara. Looks like you missed your flight again," she said without rancor.

Cara raised both hands in a gesture of surrender. "Zarah? Why are you pointing a gun at my father?"

"Hey, now, no one said anything about pointin' guns at

people," Paul Stanton said, his forced laugh ringing hollow in the tense room.

The other woman hitched her shoulder in a shrug. "I needed to get your attention."

"Okay. You've got it," Cara said. "Can you lower the gun now?"

She fixated on the semiautomatic pistol in the woman's hand. It was strange to see a gun out in the open after living in Southern California for so long. She wasn't far into her freshman year when she learned to keep her mouth shut about horses, heifers and handguns. Almost everyone she knew was virulently anti-gun. Everyone except Zarah, apparently. Thankfully, the other woman complied.

She choked down the sob of relief squeezing her throat. "You okay, Daddy?"

"I'm fine, sugar," her father responded, his voice even and steady. "Got work to do, though. Not that *he* would know a darn thing about an honest day's labor," he added, jerking his chin in Paul Stanton's direction.

"Hey, now—" Stanton began, grabbing hold of his tooled leather belt and hiking his pants as he stepped forward.

"How dare you, Paul Stanton?" Betsy Beckett said in a low, tremulous voice. "What kind of trouble have you brought into my home?"

"Elizabeth, I swear—" Stanton began, but Cara raised a hand to stop him.

"We can get into the hows and whys later." Turning to Zarah, she scowled at the gun then the sharp-featured young woman who held it. "What do you want?"

"I want what everyone wants," Zarah said as if the answer should have been obvious. "I want what people have been telling you for weeks. I want you out."

"What's it to you?" Cara shot back.

With a huff of impatience, Zarah rolled her eyes. "Oh, I plan to have a vested interest."

Cara looked everywhere but at the back door. The last thing she wanted to do was tip Zarah off to Wyatt's imminent arrival. She took in the familiar kitchen, the ancient wood napkin holder bracketed by salt and pepper shakers, the iron skillet wiped clean and waiting on the stovetop, the café curtains Grandma June had helped her make for a Mother's Day gift.

The refrigerator's compressor hummed, undercutting the tension in the room. Drawing a steadying breath, Cara forced herself to meet Zarah's gaze. "What interest?"

"She said she's engaged to Tom Wasinski," Paul Stanton chimed in. When her mother shot him a filthy look, the man took an involuntary step back. "I'm sorry, Elizabeth, but Wasinski could be a deep-pockets donor and if I run for Senate, I want him on my side. His company is about to go public."

The Beckett family turned to glare at him as one. If her expression was one-tenth as incredulous as her father's, Paul Stanton had to feel lower than an earthworm.

"I always knew you were about as stiff as a fence post, Stanton, but I never realized you were as dense as one," Jim Beckett grumbled. "Our Cara is an equal partner in their company. Her pockets are every bit as deep as either of those two fellas."

"Now, Jim," Betsy began, long accustomed to stepping between the two men.

"Not for long," Zarah said. She pointed the muzzle of the gun to a plain manila folder on the small dining table. "Cara's about to get out of the business."

Cara wanted to bask in the warmth of her father's pride, but the glint of sunlight off gunmetal made it difficult to enjoy the moment. "You are not engaged to Tom," she said flatly.

"Well, not technically engaged," Zarah conceded. "But once you sign these papers, I'll be able to hook up with him, you know, as an equal, and he won't have to worry about whether he's 'technically' connected to my employment," she said, using a single set of air quotes to dismiss the excuse Tom must have used to rebuff her.

But Cara knew the two weren't and never had been involved. In one of the few confidences they'd shared recently, Tom had confessed he was deeply, but quietly, involved with a woman he'd met on a tech-free weekend yoga retreat he'd attended months ago. One Cara herself had recommended and Zarah had booked. Could it be the mystery woman in Tom's life actually was Zarah? She racked her memory for a name, but couldn't recall him disclosing one.

Cara wondered if she'd missed something big in her old friend's life, or if the young woman she'd trusted with hers was delusional.

"How long have you and Tom been involved?" she asked, her approach cautious.

"We talk all the time." Zarah smiled smugly, pulling her long ponytail over her shoulder with her free hand and stroking it as if she was settling in for some girl talk rather than holding Cara's loved ones at gunpoint. "I know he feels like he can't let things evolve as they stand now, but together, we're going to take LYYF to the next level."

Cara could only hope Zarah had forgotten there was a special agent with the Arkansas State Police staying with them.

"What about Chris?" Cara asked, anxious to keep her engaged.

"Chris won't be a problem. Everyone knows he's going to take the money and run the minute he can cash in." She tipped her chin up. "You and Chris never cared about what it took to keep the company going. Tom is the brains behind it all."

"Tom doesn't create content," Cara pointed out.

Zarah gave an indelicate snort. "Like it's difficult." She rolled her eyes. "I've been helping you churn that stuff out for years. Besides, I'm a better actress. I've booked more roles than you have in half the time in Hollywood."

"I talked to you this morning," Cara said, stalling for time. "How did you get here so fast?"

The younger woman rolled her eyes. "It's not like it was difficult to figure out you were stalling. Plus, TSA's system is ridiculously easy to hack. I've been waiting to see if you boarded a plane going anywhere. When you changed your flight, I booked one to Dallas. When you didn't turn up, I hopped a flight to Springfield, Missouri, and drove down." She pursed her lips. "I guess it's pretty enough with the trees and all, but there's not much around here." She wrinkled her nose in distaste. "And it's so run-down." She glanced over at Paul Stanton. "You might get more people to visit if things didn't look so...poor."

Paul opened his mouth to protest, but Cara spoke first. "So what do you expect to happen here today?"

Without missing a beat, Zarah pointed the gun at Cara's mother's chest. "I expect you to sign over your partnership."

Her father half rose from his chair and Paul Stanton bumbled forward with a hearty "Hey, now—"

Zarah swung the gun from one man to the other and they both subsided, hands raised. Moving closer to the table, Cara placed herself between Zarah and her mother. She was the target here, not her parents. Cara had to make certain Zarah kept her eye on the prize.

"Who am I signing it over to? You?" Cara asked, trying to keep her tone curious rather than accusatory.

"Yes. Sign it over to me, and I will let Tom know we can be together now. Equal partners," Zarah said with a decisive nod. Her pretty face brightened. "I mean, it's not like this is what you wanted to do with your life, right? And if you still want to be involved, maybe we can pay you a salary or something."

Cara glanced down to see her father staring at her intently. He cut his eyes to the window, and it was all she could do to keep from looking over. Wyatt must be out there. *Please let him be out there.* She needed to buy time.

"It was you, wasn't it?" she said softly.

"What was?" Zarah asked, squinting as if confused by the non sequitur.

"All of it. The doxing. The messages. All the...stuff." She closed her eyes, willing herself to hold it together as the pieces fell into place. "You did it."

"Oh, that," Zarah said with a dismissive laugh. She shrugged. "I put some info out there, but the rest... I didn't have to do much."

"Except have me kidnapped," Cara interjected.

"Oh, well, technically, you paid for that yourself. Good thing you never look at your account statements, huh?" She wrinkled her nose. "Anyway, didn't go as expected. He was only supposed to take you somewhere and scare you into signing."

"Now he's dead," Cara said flatly.

"Yeah, well, not my fault. He shouldn't have taken the job if he couldn't handle the pressure." Zarah exhaled in a put-upon whoosh. "I guess I learned a good lesson on outsourcing."

Cara fixated on the gun dangling from Zarah's hand like

an afterthought. She didn't look like she had much experience handling firearms. She certainly hadn't been taught how to handle one safely. She was waving what looked like a small nine millimeter around like it was a water pistol. And what if Wyatt came through the door and startled her? She could accidentally shoot any one of them.

Drawing on every acting lesson she'd ever had, Cara forced herself to look into Zarah's eyes with what she hoped were eyes filled with hope and optimism. "You know this was never what I expected to do with my life," she began, faking a quaver into her voice. "I don't know how I got this far off track." She bumped her mother with her hip, signaling the older woman to scoot her chair away. She pointed to the folder on the table. "What is this?"

"It's an agreement to transfer your partnership shares," Zarah said, her customary chipper efficiency slipping back into place. "And you've always been really nice to work with, Cara. I'm not going to leave you high and dry. Once the public offering goes through and prices are up, I'll cover you. In today's cash value, of course," she added.

"Of course," Cara murmured.

Out front, Roscoe gave a woof of greeting and they all turned. Zarah swung the gun around when a floorboard creaked. "Sounds like your hot cop is still hanging around after all," she said, turning back to press the muzzle into the dusty folds of her father's Carhartt jacket. "Tell him to join us," she called out in a louder voice. "But be sure to tell him I'm holding your sweet daddy at gunpoint."

"Wyatt, if that's you, Zarah is here and she has a gun," Cara called out robotically.

"I'm coming in, and I am *not* holding a gun," he announced before stepping into the doorway, his hands raised. To Cara's disappointment, he wasn't lying. There was no sign of a weapon in Special Agent Wyatt Dawson's hand.

"Some cop you got yourself there," Zarah scoffed. "He's got a kind of hot-nerd vibe going on. Too bad he couldn't come in busting down the doors to save you."

Cara raised her eyebrows. "He's a cybercrime guy. I'm not sure kicking in doors is their thing. He tells me they barely leave the office."

She shot Wyatt an apologetic glance and he made a point of scowling at her. But the glint in his eyes was keen and bright. He wasn't insulted, nor did he seem to be worried. Which made exactly one of them. Had he somehow called for backup? How long would it take someone to get there? Their eyes held for a moment and a veil of calm settled around her shoulders. He wasn't freaking out over a woman who was clearly suffering some sort of break waving a very real gun around like a toy. She wouldn't either.

"So what's the situation?" Wyatt asked, his tone casual, almost disinterested.

"We're talking business," Zarah snapped.

"Talking business with a gun pointed at a person?" Wyatt asked smoothly. "Isn't asking someone to sign legal documents at gunpoint coercion?"

Cara shot him a quelling look. "Don't you worry about it. Wasn't I telling you I was thinking about doing something different with my career? Well, Zarah is here and we're talking about making a deal."

"A deal in which she fronts zero dollars, and you sign everything over?" her father asked with an incredulous laugh.

"I'm going to pay her once the stock offering is complete. Tom and I can combine our shares, pay Cara for her time and efforts to this point and still have controlling interest in the company."

"Sounds like you have it all figured out." Cara nudged her mother with her knee, but Betsy didn't budge. "Mama, you still keep extra pens in your junk drawer?"

When she looked down, her mother was staring at her with naked disbelief. When she spoke, all traces of syrupy sweetness were long gone from Betsy Beckett's voice. "You can't seriously be considering signing those papers."

Cara shifted so Zarah couldn't see the silent stare-down between her and her mother. "Mama, I know what I'm doing." She thought of the old handgun her granddad kept in the kitchen drawer of the old house. Cara knew it made the move to this one along with Grandma June's cast-iron skillet. She'd seen it in the back of the junk drawer. "I know you and Daddy have never approved of what I do. Here's my chance to start over. I can have all my time back to pursue acting…real acting. All I need to do is sign on the dotted line and this will be all over."

"How do we know?" Betsy demanded. "How do we know she won't shoot us all?"

Zarah looked aghast at the suggestion. "You think I like doing this? I hate it. I'm not one of you hillbilly gun nuts," she snarled. "All I want is my share of LYYF and I'll be out of here."

Cara grabbed the folder again and waved it like a flag of surrender. "Fine. You know what? I'm tired of this. I want my life back. My actual life-life. The one I plan on living." She flipped over the folder and dumped the papers out onto the table.

She took the seat across from her father and Zarah and pulled the papers closer. "Mama, please grab me a pen, would you? If I know you, you've got at least six or seven of them you swiped from Buck's stashed in there," she said, naming a local gunsmith's shop.

It was both a request and a prod. The moment she met her mother's fiery gaze she knew the message had been received. With a small nod, Betsy rose and walked stiffly to the drawer on the far side of the stove.

It was time to show her know-it-all assistant from California how hillbillies from run-down little towns in the Ozarks settled their disputes.

She pretended to reread the first page of the documents, her shoulders tensing as she heard her mother rustling through the drawer behind her. "So, how will you work the transfer of funds?" she asked, pitching her voice low so Zarah would be forced to focus on her.

"Crypto?" the other woman replied with a cheeky smile.

Cara snorted. "Nope. Cash."

"I'll wire transfer it to you." Zarah flashed a dimpling smile. "It'll be easy. I already know all your account numbers."

"Yeah, I may need to rework some of those things," Cara murmured, keeping her head down as the rummaging continued behind her. "Mama? You find me a pen?"

"Hold your horses. I'm looking for one that works." To emphasize her point, Betsy tossed a cheap plastic ballpoint to the floor in disgust. "I have got to clean this mess out one day."

"Sounds like you need an assistant, Mrs. Beckett," Zarah chirped.

"Maybe so," her mother murmured. The sifting of clutter finally ceased, and Cara glanced over her shoulder to see her mother reach up and carefully tuck her hair behind her ear, clearing her peripheral vision. "I'm not finding a decent ink pen, but I did find this."

With one fluid move, Betsy Beckett swung around to face the young woman, her father-in-law's old service pistol in her hand and a grim expression hardening her pretty features. "Drop the gun."

Zarah's eyes widened. "No," she snapped, jabbing her gun into Jim Beckett's ribs so hard he let out a soft grunt. "This is my plan. We're going to do things my way," she insisted, her voice climbing with agitation.

"Oh, God," Paul Stanton blurted. Both of his arms raised, he turned toward the front door. Seeing Wyatt in the doorway, he stopped short. "This is too much. It's all too far out of hand."

"You think?" Wyatt asked, unperturbed.

Cara looked up as the lieutenant governor switched directions, then dithered, his arms flailing. "I have to get out of here. I can't be here. I was never here," he babbled.

"Could have sworn I saw you," Wyatt replied, his voice a life preserver of quiet and calm amid the melee.

"I can have your badge," Paul Stanton threatened, spittle flying from his mouth.

"You can try," Wyatt challenged. "But from where I'm standing, it doesn't look good for you, Mr. Stanton."

"You drop your gun," Zarah demanded, stepping back from Cara's father and training her sights on Betsy instead.

You chose incorrectly, Cara thought as her mother released the safety on her weapon.

"You terrorize my daughter, point a gun at my husband and track your muddy shoes on my kitchen floor and you think you get to give the orders here?" Betsy demanded, widening her stance. "I don't think so, honey."

Out of the corner of her eye Cara saw Wyatt lowering his hands. He was cool as a cucumber. It gave her the confidence she needed to end this farce once and for all.

Meeting Zarah's eyes, she spoke slowly and deliberately.

"Lower the gun now, or I will never sign this. Mama, you too," she added. "I mean it. Everyone, lower the guns now."

"You mean everyone but me, right?" Wyatt asked, drawing his weapon from its holster at the small of his back as he closed the distance between him and Zarah.

Zarah's head whipped around in surprise, but his aim didn't waver as he took hold of her wrist with his left hand, expertly squeezing at the precise pressure point to make her release her grip. The gun she'd been waving around dropped to the floor as he twisted her arm behind her back.

"Zarah Parvich, you are under arrest. You have the right…"

Cara sat frozen, unable to tear her gaze away from the sight of Wyatt holding both of Zarah's empty hands behind her back.

"Cara, can I ask a favor?" Wyatt asked politely.

"Uh-huh," she said, and nodded.

"I left my coat on the living room floor. I have some zip tie restraints in the inside pocket. Grab a couple for me?"

"Sure," she replied as she rose.

"I'm leaving," Paul Stanton announced.

He took two steps toward the front room and without thinking, Cara snatched Grandma June's skillet from the stovetop and swung. She aimed for his body and not his head, wanting to slow the man, not kill him.

But the lieutenant governor wasn't the least bit grateful for her forethought. Cursing a blue streak, Stanton fell against the fridge, then crumpled to the floor, clutching his right arm.

"Excuse me, Uncle Paul," she said with a sneer as she stepped over his legs. "I think we'd like you to stay a bit longer."

On the opposite side of the room, Jim jumped up from his

chair and hurried to embrace his wife. "Girl didn't know who she was messing with," he murmured into her hair.

Her mother gave a watery laugh. "I'm a regular Dirty Harriet," she said, burrowing in.

Cara carried Wyatt's coat back into the kitchen and her mother looked up, shaking her head. "Holy cow, girl, I can't believe you remembered this gun." Betsy wiped her eyes with the heels of her hands. "I doubt it's had a bullet in the chamber in the last twenty years. How did you know it was still there?"

"I saw it the other day when I was looking for a pen," Cara said with a smirk. "You've got everything in the world in there except a working ink pen." Holding Wyatt's jacket by the collar, she turned her attention to him. "What are you carrying in here? It weighs a ton."

"Nothing much. Flashlight, pepper spray, flex cuffs, extra magazines, a collapsible baton," he said offhandedly. "Standard desk jockey stuff."

She pulled two zip ties from the deep inner pocket and handed one over. Zarah stood, unresisting, her head bowed, her lips clamped shut. Once she was cuffed, Wyatt guided her to a spot on the floor against the wall where she sat silently weeping.

Cara watched as he used the end of the other plastic strap to pick the discarded gun up off the floor. He deposited the weapon on the kitchen table, then looked from Cara to the woman on the tile floor.

"I called for backup from state police and the sheriff's department before I came inside. They should be here shortly. You okay to keep an eye on her while I see to our esteemed lieutenant governor?" he asked.

"I am," Cara responded. And to her surprise, it was true.

Lowering herself to the floor in front of the woman who'd turned her world upside down, she whispered, "Okay. Okay. Easy. Deep breaths, Zarah. Breathe in…"

Chapter Fifteen

Within minutes, her parents' house was a complete circus. Teams from both the state police and the Searcy County Sheriff's Office jostled for jurisdiction, but everyone knew in the end the county would have to give way.

"I knew I should have checked your financials," Wyatt muttered.

"Most people don't hire their own kidnappers," she murmured, her gaze fixed on her former assistant.

"Would have saved a lot of time and grief," he replied.

"Next time," she promised.

They watched as Zarah was properly secured and led to one of the trooper's vehicles for transport to Little Rock. A short distance away, Cara's mother stood behind the EMT checking Paul Stanton's arm to ascertain whether X-rays might be needed, reading her onetime prom date the proverbial riot act. Her father stood off to one side, a faint smile curving his mouth, his admiring gaze locked on his wife.

"She's something," Wyatt said to her father. "Nearly gave me a heart attack when she pulled a gun out of her kitchen drawer."

Jim Beckett looped an arm over Cara's shoulders and tucked her into his embrace.

"My dad didn't like leaving my mother in the house alone

while he was out doing chores, but as he used to say, you can't keep the inside and the outside up at the same time. So, he kept his old service pistol in the kitchen drawer in case trouble came strolling up the road. She must have brought it with her when she moved in with us."

"She did," Cara said quietly. "She told me Granddad would want us to have it to hand."

Without peeling his eyes off the floor show, her father pressed a kiss to the side of her head in a gesture he hadn't made in years, but one she remembered so well it brought a hot rush of tears to Cara's eyes.

"And another thing, Paul Anthony Stanton," her mother said, shaking her finger in the face of the man who held the second-most-powerful office in the state. "The minute they haul you out of here, I'm not only calling your precious mama, but I'm also callin' Delia Raitt. By the time I'm done with you, you won't be able to get elected prom king in prison or dogcatcher anywhere else!"

"I know I should stop her, but it's so darn entertaining," her father murmured to no one in particular. "Better than any show on CineFlix."

"Agent Dawson?" A shorter, powerfully built man with a blankly sober expression stood in the doorway Wyatt had filled mere hours before. "Could we speak to you in private, please?"

Wyatt nodded. "Yes, sir." He glanced first at Cara, then her father. "Y'all okay here?"

"We'll be fine," her father replied, giving her a squeeze as he answered for both of them.

Wyatt hesitated, his gaze lingering on her. Her cheeks heated, but thankfully, her father remained enthralled by the dressing down her mother hadn't quite wrapped up. "I'm good. Go do what you do," she said with a little jerk of her chin.

When he was gone, her father said, "I like him. Decent guy."

"I do too," Cara said quietly.

Satisfied with what he found, the EMT turned to one of the troopers standing nearby. "Doesn't look to be broken, but he should have an X-ray to be sure there's no fracture."

"Too bad," Jim whispered to Cara as the troopers hauled the man up from the chair and out of their house. "Swing for the fences next time, sugar."

She giggled and gave him a playful elbow jab. "Daddy. Behave." She assumed a prim expression. "You know I'm a pacifist."

He pulled back enough to tuck his chin to his chest and glare at her. "What? You only eat fish caught in the Pacific?"

She rolled her eyes and groaned. "Even for a dad joke that was bad."

Betsy Beckett turned to face them, hands planted on her hips. Thankfully, she seemed to have expended her supply of vitriol. "What's so funny, you two?"

"Not Dad's jokes," Cara replied. She slid out from under her father's arm and hugged her mother. "You were fantastic today."

"I guess I learned more than I thought I had, watchin' all those depressing shows your daddy likes."

"I wasn't worried. I know my wife." He leaned in and pressed a smacking kiss to Betsy's lips. "She can take care of herself and everyone else around her." He turned and looked at Cara as he pulled on the heavy work jacket he'd shrugged out of when the first of the patrol cars arrived. "You get it from her, Care Bear. You're like your mama."

A lump the size of a boulder rose in Cara's throat.

"Where do you think you're going?" her mother demanded as he reached for the handle on the back door. "I have a house full of cops and robbers here, and the police are going to want to talk to you some more. If you think you're going to slink off—"

"I'm goin' to see to the feed. I'll be right back," he said, zipping the jacket up to his chin.

He was gone before either of them could say another word. Betsy exhaled an exasperated sigh. "I swear he breaks out in hives if he has to spend more than an hour of daylight indoors."

"Probably," Cara concurred. "Nothing new there." A crime scene team bustled in, and it quickly became clear they were in the way. She caught her mother's tired gaze. "Let's go in the other room?"

"Sounds good," Betsy replied.

But when they slipped into the living room, they found themselves caught in the cross fire between one of the sheriff's men and an officious-looking state trooper. Betsy steered them toward the dining room, but there they found several men and a young woman dressed in dark suits setting up laptops and pulling legal pads from briefcases. Before they could be spotted, Cara took her mother's hand and led her down the hall toward the bedrooms. She could hear the rumble of deep voices coming from the room Wyatt had been using, so they tiptoed down the hall into Cara's room, closing the door silently behind them.

Betsy leaned against the closed door as if bracing against an approaching horde. "Good gracious, there's a lot of people in my house," Betsy said, patting her chest. "I hope they don't look too close at my floors. I haven't swept in days and Roscoe sheds enough for us to build a brand-new dog twice a week."

"Poor Roscoe," Cara said, peeking out her window at the front porch. Close to a dozen patrol cars and SUVs were parked haphazardly in the driveway and on the lawn, and the poor old dog had felt duty bound to greet every one of them. "I hope he's—" She scanned the porch until she spotted a familiar lump parked next to the rail. "Good, he's sleeping." She let the blind fall back into place with a chortle. "Wouldn't want him missing his middle-late-afternoon-pre-supper snooze."

"Supper," her mother groaned, stepping away from the door and dropping heavily onto the side of the single bed Cara had dutifully made before leaving the house.

Dropping down beside her mother, Cara patted her knee. "I think we're going to open the fridge and call whatever falls out supper."

Betsy tipped her head onto Cara's shoulder, and the simple reversal of their usual roles made Cara feel more centered than she had in years.

"Mama?"

"Hmm?"

"I think I am going to sell," Cara said, the words coming out as the thought took hold.

Her mother didn't move a muscle. For a moment, Cara wondered if Betsy had fallen asleep, or simply hadn't heard her, but then she stirred. Sitting up, she took both of Cara's hands in hers and held them tight as she gazed deep into her eyes.

"Don't decide anything now. Whatever you do, you do it in your time and in your way. No matter what anyone says, you created something special. You created it. You are the one who gets to decide what's right for you, and your creation."

"Well, me and Chris and Tom," Cara said with a self-deprecating little laugh.

"No, Cara," her mother said, giving her hands a squeeze. "Only you. Partners can help and support each other, but they can't dictate how we live our lives. You can walk with them, follow your own path or figure out a way to blaze a whole new trail. Make sure, in the end, you choose which it will be." Her mother let go long enough to sweep Cara's hair from her brow. "I imagine it's like a marriage. You have to be your own person, but together. Every day, choosing to be together."

Cara gave a snort of a laugh. "If my business partnership were a marriage, it would be illegal in most states."

Betsy rolled her eyes. "You know what I am saying. I'm only saying not to make any big moves until after this whole stock thingamajig is done. I have no idea if those fellas you're working with were actually involved in all of this mess or not, but I say let the truth come to light. You hang on and get everything you have coming to you, because it's yours and you earned it. After, well, then you can make your choices and your daddy and I will support you. One hundred percent."

Cara flung herself into her mother's arms. "Thank you, Mama."

They rocked as they held one another, Betsy alternately humming and shushing her. Cara was so happy to be assured of her parents' approbation to worry about the mixed messages.

With a snuffle, Cara pulled back a bit. Her gaze landed on the boy-band poster. "Mama, why didn't you ever take that poster down?"

Betsy spared the yellowing print a half glance, then pulled Cara close again. "As long as I kept it up, we'd both know this would always be your room. Whenever you came home, you'd feel…at home."

Cara squeezed her mother tight again and they stayed locked together until someone rapped lightly on the door.

"Who's there?" Cara said, dashing fingertips under her damp eyes.

"It's Wyatt," he replied without attempting to open the door. "Are all three of you hiding in there?"

Cara and Betsy laughed. "Jim has gone out to be with his cows," Betsy called back.

When he still didn't open the door, Cara asked, "You want to hide out in here too?"

The door opened slowly, and Wyatt poked his head in, a sheepish smile crinkling his eyes. "Hey."

"Hi," Cara returned, a single eyebrow raised. "You in or you out?"

His smile dissolved into a wince, and he raised a hand to the back of his neck in a gesture so familiar to her now, it made her chest ache. His gaze dropped to the floor and he shifted his weight from one foot to the other. "Listen, Emma is here with some guys from the FBI and the Department of Justice. It looks like we're talking state and federal charges for, uh, well, both of them and they want to talk to you."

"Okay." Cara rose, smoothing her hands down the front of the jeans she'd been so happy to acquire earlier in this endless day. "Let's do it."

Wyatt took a small step back, then glanced down the hall before turning back to her with an apologetic smile. "Actually, I have to go."

"Go?" she and her mother asked in unison.

Then Cara noticed the packed duffel at his feet. "Oh."

"The guy I was talking to is my section chief, Simon Taylor. He's heading back to Little Rock now and wants me to give him my full report on the way."

"Oh," Cara repeated, the bottom dropping out of her stomach. "Should I...? I'd like to meet him. Thank him."

Wyatt shook his head. "No need. Plus, he's not exactly

a people person, you know?" He wrinkled his nose. "Trust me, you aren't missing anything."

The silence stretched several seconds too long. Thankfully, her mother stepped into the breach. "Jim and I can't thank you enough for all you've done," she said as she rose to say her goodbyes. "Let me call him in from the barn—"

"Oh, no. Thank you, ma'am," Wyatt said with a quick, hard shake of his head. "I didn't do much more than try to tug on a few loose threads."

Her mother wrapped an arm around Cara's waist and gave her an encouraging squeeze. "You brought our daughter home safely to us."

Wyatt met Cara's eyes at last, then gave her a lopsided smile. "No. I didn't even do that. Jim was right. Cara took care of herself and everyone else around her. I was nothing more than the guy who got to drive her home."

"Dawson?" a man called from down the hall.

"I have to go." Wyatt raised a hand in farewell. "Take care, okay?" He gave her a winsome smile. "Make sure the guys let you be the one who rings the big bell next week. You deserve it."

He turned away, hoisting his bag onto his shoulder in one fluid move. Cara and her mother followed him down the hall, but stopped short of the living room. Wyatt didn't seem to want to linger. The stern-looking man holding a leather computer bag nodded to her and her mother, then followed his agent—her agent—out the front door.

Cara wanted to call after him, but she couldn't make any sound come out. Besides, what could she say? He was with his boss. She was with her mother. Surely they'd have a chance to catch up later. She sucked in a breath when he stopped to give Roscoe a pat as the other man made a bee-line for a marked state police SUV.

"Ms. Beckett?" the young redhead she'd seen setting up equipment said as she strode toward them, her hand extended. "Special Agent Emma Parker. It's good to meet you in person."

"Oh. Yes. Emma." Cara mustered her best smile, but knew it probably came across several watts weaker than usual. "Thank you for all you've been doing for the case." She gestured to her mother. "This is my mom, Elizabeth Beckett."

"Betsy," her mother supplied as the two women shook hands.

"If you don't mind, we'd like to ask you a few more questions," Emma said, gesturing to the dining room. "Wyatt said it would be okay for us to set up in your dining room, Mrs. Beckett, but I promise we'll be out of your hair ASAP."

Cara stiffened as a flash of headlights strafed the front of the house. She blinked a couple times, then saw the taillights on the SUV flash bright as the driver tapped the brakes. Her heart lurched. For a second, she thought maybe Wyatt had forgotten something and was coming back. Maybe the thing he'd forgotten was her.

Then she saw the vehicle dip as the driver maneuvered onto the rutted gravel lane and picked up speed.

"You go on with Agent Parker," her mother said in a gentle tone. "Do what you need to do. I'll fix up a mess of sandwiches for whoever wants something." Cara hesitated and her mother leaned in to kiss her cheek. "Go on now. Maybe later I'll tell you about the guy who drove me home from the prom."

Cara took a half step away before her mother's teaser fully registered. "Drove you home from the prom? You said you went to prom with Paul Stanton," she said with a puzzled frown.

"I did," Betsy said, a serene smile curving her lips. "I went with Paul. Danced with him a couple times too, but he was more interested in sneaking drinks with his football buddies." Her smile turned enigmatic as she started toward the kitchen. "Your daddy was the one who drove me home. It's been him ever since."

Epilogue

Cara Beckett strolled through Arrivals at Bill and Hillary Clinton National Airport without a single person recognizing her, and that was exactly the way she liked it. She tossed a glance over her shoulder to be sure her companions were right behind her.

"You're in the fast-paced capital city now. Try to keep up," she called over her shoulder.

"There's seriously only one terminal?" Chris asked, quickening his pace to fall in beside her.

"Yep."

She smiled as they approached the single escalator down to the baggage claim area. Cara paused to allow Chris to go first, waiting for Tom to catch up. With his ever-present computer bag hanging off one shoulder and a small carry-on in the other hand, the man was craning his neck as if the small airport was one of the wonders of the modern world.

"Come on, Captain Moneybags, you can put an offer in on the place another time," she teased.

"It's weird. I guess I've only ever flown into larger airports," he observed, stepping on the escalator behind her.

"When you've flown commercial," she qualified. "We won't count general aviation."

Tom frowned as he pondered her take. "You know, if

you're serious about this, maybe we should look into investing in a company plane after all," he mused.

"Yes!" Chris thrust his fist into the air, garnering the attention of the passengers around them. He didn't shrink from the spotlight. "I've been saying so for years."

"Yeah, well, we haven't been able to actually afford one," Tom shot back.

"And now we can," Chris said, his smile smug.

At the foot of the escalator he hooked a hand through Cara's arm. Tom flanked her left side, and they walked three abreast through the sliding doors into bright autumn sunshine. The late-November breeze swirled around them.

Beside her Chris gave an exaggerated shudder. "I thought it was supposed to be hot in the South?" he complained.

"We're due east of Los Angeles," she reminded him.

"Do I need to call a car?" Tom said, sliding a phone from his pocket.

"No, I have a friend picking us up," she said as she scanned the line of cars depositing and scooping up passengers. She spotted the plain black SUV with the state tags parked in one of the diagonal pull-through spots with a five-minute limit. "There she is."

As they approached, the driver's door opened and Emma Parker stepped out. "You made it," she said, meeting them at the back of the vehicle.

"We made it," Cara called back. "Tom, Chris, this is Special Agent Emma Parker. Be polite. She has a gun."

But it was Emma who was enthralled by the sight of the tech whizzes. "Wow. I'm so thrilled to meet you." She shook each man's hand, then turned to Tom. "I've been hacking multiplayer games since I was eleven. Like you." A pretty peach blush colored her cheeks. "I mean, I know you used to—"

Tom cut her off there. "Don't tell anyone, but sometimes I still do."

"He never had the patience to beat them legitimately," Chris chimed in.

"Me either," Emma said with a grin.

"Some of us actually have skills," Chris said pointedly.

"Okay, okay." Cara waved them both toward the doors. "You can flirt with her while we drive."

Once they were all settled into the vehicle, Emma joined the steady flow of traffic circling the small airport. Cara pointed to the parking deck. "The garage where I got carjacked," she said, using her best impression of a tour guide.

"Not funny," Tom muttered.

"I'm not kidding," she retorted.

"Cara's Trauma Tours," Chris said with a peevish edge. "Not a great selling point for your plan."

Cara turned and found both men scowling at the concrete structure as if it were responsible for the incident. "I don't have to sell you on my plan," she reminded them gently.

"We're still partners," Tom argued.

Smiling, Cara nodded, pleased too with the way they'd reconnected in the two weeks since Zarah Parvich and Paul Stanton were arrested and LYYF had a record-breaking launch on the stock exchange. When Cara told them she was heading back to Arkansas to spend Thanksgiving with her parents, the two men seemed genuinely sad to end the ongoing celebration.

"I can tell you the whole cybercrimes crew is really excited to have you drop by," Emma informed them as they merged onto the highway. She shot Cara a sidelong glance. "Wyatt in particular."

"Well, we appreciate all you did to help Cara," Chris answered. "A quick stopover to thank you in person is the least we could do."

Cara watched the highway signs zip past. This was the same route Gerald Griffin had forced her to take mere weeks before, but looked completely different with her two oldest friends along for the ride. Just a few miles down, Emma signaled her intent to exit. Arkansas State Police Headquarters was located in an old shopping mall on the city's south side.

Within minutes, Emma had wheeled the SUV into a spot designated for official vehicles and killed the engine. "We've got about an hour before I'll need to get you back to check in for your flights out."

"Let's do this then," Chris said, reaching for the door handle and discovering it was useless. He was trapped in the back of the police SUV. "Or not."

"Cop locks," Emma informed them. "Hang on, we'll let you out."

"Yeah. Makes sense," Chris muttered as Emma opened the rear door for him.

Cara smiled at Tom as he stepped out of the vehicle.

"Should I take my bags?" he asked.

Emma wrinkled her nose, then shrugged. "Up to you. This is not a great area, but if they're not safe in this vehicle, they aren't safe in any."

"Good point."

Emma made a point of chirping the locks as they walked away, and they all laughed.

A chuckle tangled in Cara's throat when one of the glass doors leading into headquarters opened and Wyatt Dawson stepped into the sunlight. His hair glinted gold and his shoulders looked broader than ever as he crossed his arms over his chest and waited for them, his lips curved into a smile he was clearly keeping on a tight rein.

Cara hung back, allowing Emma to make the introductions between the men. When Wyatt reached for the door and held it open for them, she hesitated on the sidewalk. Wyatt clocked her position with a glance, then let the door swing shut behind the others.

"Hey," he said, his gaze locked on her.

"Hi," she returned.

Then, unable to hold back a moment longer, Cara flung herself at him. He caught her up easily, strong arms winding tight around her as she buried her face in his neck.

"One minute you were there, and before I could even… you were gone," she mumbled into his skin.

"I wanted to stay. I wanted to stay with you, but I didn't know what you wanted and I couldn't… I love my job, Cara. I didn't know—"

"No. Right, I know," she said, her voice choked.

He held her fast, one hand sliding up her back to hold her to him even tighter. "Breathe," he whispered into her ear.

She gave a soggy chuckle and inhaled deeply. Maybe she got drunk on the scent of his soap, or perhaps he was exuding some kind of pheromone that made rational women lose their minds. She didn't know exactly why she pressed her lips to the exposed skin above his collar, she only knew it was absolutely necessary.

Wyatt froze for a second, and she wondered if she'd gone too far.

Then, the next thing she knew, he gripped the back of her head in his big, warm palm and his mouth was on hers. His lips were warm and firm, the bottom slightly chapped from his habit of gnawing on it, but all in all, the kiss was perfect. Long, lingering and packed with promise.

She pressed her slick lips together when he drew back for air. The last thing she wanted was to do something stupid like apologize. Not when she was not the least bit sorry he'd kissed her.

"I've wanted to kiss you a long time," he confessed, his voice slightly hoarse. "But this probably isn't the best time and place."

"Feels right to me," she said, her voice breathy.

"Complicates things," he said gruffly.

"Not for me," she answered, pulling back to look him in the eye. "This is by far the easiest decision I've made in weeks."

"Is it?"

She nodded. "I'm heading up to my folks for Thanksgiving," she informed him.

To her chagrin, he loosened his hold on her. "Sounds great. I'll be working on shift for the holiday, but probably head down to see my family over the weekend."

"Oh. I see."

She was unable to mask her disappointment, and he was as perceptive as ever. "Why? What's happening?"

"Oh, nothing." Cara flashed a shaky smile, her nerves ratcheting up as they circled one another. Taking a calming breath, she dove in. "I was wondering if you might have some free time this weekend."

His eyebrows rose. "Well, sure. I mean, I didn't have anything set in stone. What did you have in mind?"

"I thought you might like to come with me to check out a piece of property," she suggested, hugging herself as she braced against the stiff wind and possible rejection.

"Property?"

"There's a couple places out near Pinnacle Mountain State Park." His eyes lit with interest when she mentioned the recreational area just north and west of Little Rock. "You know, I was thinking someplace far enough out to have some land to build a studio, but close enough to enjoy the perks of high-speed internet."

"The perks of high-speed internet?" he repeated, his smile stretching wide. "What kind of perks?"

"Oh, you know, cop shows on CineFlix. And maybe, if the connection is as reliable as I think it is, a certain cop might possibly show up at my door to watch cop shows on Cine-Flix?" she suggested with a hopeful smile.

"I'd love to come look at property with you," he said, looking her square in the eye.

"I'm not going back to California," she told him. "I mean, at least not permanently. I'm sure I'll have to go out there someti—"

He cut her off with another kiss, this one swift and sure.

They jumped apart when someone hit the crash bar on the door with a little extra force. "Hey, Dawson," a gruff voice called out.

Cara laughed, pressing her forehead to Wyatt's shoulder as she tipped her head to the side. Trooper Masterson stood grinning in the open doorway, a small knot of people gathered around Chris and Tom behind him.

"You planning to hold the poor woman hostage or something? I wouldn't try it. I hear she's slippery."

Looping an arm across her shoulders, Wyatt kept her close as he turned toward the door. "Oh, I know. Cara Beckett can take care of herself and everyone else around her," he informed the older man. "Believe me, I plan to stay on her good side."

* * * * *

HARLEQUIN
Reader Service

Enjoyed your book?

Try the perfect subscription for Romance readers and get more great books like this delivered right to your door.

See why over 10+ million readers have tried Harlequin Reader Service.

Start with a Free Welcome Collection with free books and a gift—valued over $20.

Choose any series in print or ebook. See website for details and order today:

TryReaderService.com/subscriptions